Law Girl's Bump in the Road

Leia London

© 2018 Leia London
All rights reserved.

ISBN: 1983539597
ISBN 13: 9781983539596

1

"Please don't throw up," I chanted under my breath as the contents of my stomach crept up my esophagus. My rebellious stomach gurgled as the taxi continued switching lanes and halting abruptly. I glanced dubiously at Jane, who was somehow completely poised and stick straight in her seat after an overnight bus ride and a day spent scavenging in the aisles of Century 21, a massive, designer discount department store. I turned to Alex.

"I just want to warn you. I may need to throw up," I whispered loudly over the street noise and the banter from the taxi TV. "But I'll let you know."

Alex grinned, apparently assuming I was referring to our cabbie's unique driving style—until she looked at my face.

"Uh, maybe you should sit beside the door, Selena." She looked slightly uncomfortable. I couldn't blame her.

"Thanks, but I can't move. I'm scared of what will happen if I do."

"Okay," she said, forcing a reassuring smile. Alex seemed like a kind person, but I didn't know her well. We were in law school together, but we weren't in the same circle of friends, and I was slightly intimidated by her extensive vocabulary. At twenty-seven, she was a couple of years older than me, and around her I always felt like some ditz who only talked about clothes and shoes and hair—which was, of course, partly true, but I could also talk about serious things too. I hoped that Alex realized that, but I had more pressing concerns at the moment. Throwing up all over her would not be the way to prove the depth of my character.

Jane, on the other hand, was a lost cause. She'd stolen my roommate, and I couldn't for a moment pretend to understand how. Catherine and I had been perfect together until she'd decided that she couldn't live with me in third year because she was going to move in with her boyfriend, Ethan—totally against her parents' wishes, by the way, and I was surprised by her decision to act out. So not like her. Anyway, during my first week back at school, I'd learned that Catherine was living with Jane! And Jane

LAW GIRL'S BUMP IN THE ROAD

was not Ethan. I couldn't help but wonder if she'd told me she was moving in with Ethan only so that she could ditch me to move in with Jane. But why stick-up-her-butt Jane? I guess they were a lot alike, but I'd always felt like Catherine and I got along because her sister and I were so similar. Who wouldn't want to live with her sister?

Well, maybe I had my answer. But obviously I couldn't show any sign of weakness in front of Jane.

Thankfully our taxi soon arrived at the restaurant where we had a dinner reservation for fifteen. It was our annual law school trip to New York City, and I'd managed to score a last-minute ticket from Catherine—who, ironically, was there on a romantic weekend with Ethan. Ethan had shelled out for a plane ticket and their own room so they wouldn't have to suffer the indignity of a ten-hour bus ride and a room shared with three other hungover people, which meant I got to. And it meant Alex and Jane were my roommates. But hey, at least I was in New York, right?

While we waited for everyone else to arrive, Alex reviewed the wine list. My stomach gurgled at the thought of wine, but I wanted something too. I couldn't just sit on a barstool and jealously look at everyone else's drink. Hmm, maybe a gin and tonic to settle my stomach. So yummy. First, though, I had to pee.

That gin and tonic apparently helped, because after we were seated, and I had devoured the complimentary focaccia, my stomach had settled down, so I split a bottle of wine with Alex and Jane. By the time dinner arrived, we had almost finished the bottle, and the nausea had been replaced by a warm, tingly sensation.

"Wait," said Alex when I returned from a visit to the washroom. "I thought you said you weren't coming on the trip this year."

"I wasn't," I admitted. "That bus ride is a killer on my neck. But then everyone was so excited, and Stephanie was coming, so I couldn't bear to be left out."

Stephanie was my best friend, but she'd decided to complete her final year of law school in Vancouver—that traitor. Still, she'd flown all the way across the country to go on the trip, so when she'd called me the night before the trip to tell me she was in town, drinking chocolate martinis and helping our other bestie, Jade, pack, I was torn. Go on the trip and end up at the chiropractor, or stay home and miss out on all the fun?

Stephanie, hearing her name, winked at me from down the table. This was so worth a visit to the chiropractor. This was going to be the best trip yet.

Of course, the lead-up to the trip had been a little crazy. By the time I'd decided to go, the tickets had been sold out, so I'd put a frantic message on the law school chat asking if anyone wanted to sell his or her ticket. Catherine and Ethan had come through for me at literally the last minute, so I'd tossed a random selection of clothing in a suitcase, thrown on my Lulus, and dashed for the bus. At which point I'd realized I'd forgotten to do something ever so slightly crucial: to tell my husband that I was going.

Right, that guy. I had mentioned it to Sam, actually. After I'd joined the girls for chocolate martinis, feeling nostalgic for the fun but not the memories of sore necks past, I'd suggested to him that maybe he and I could drive down so I could still go without being crammed into a bus seat. It would've been great. He's always the perfect gentlemen: he hails the cabs, holds the doors, and protects my friends from creepy men at clubs. I think that growing up with two sisters taught him how to take care of women. He once told me that as a kid he'd sometimes flipped through his sisters' magazines, particularly those with headlines like "The Top Three Positions Women *Really* Want." I was eternally grateful.

Sam, however, had been annoyed. He was out of town, working at some new property his parents had recently acquired.

"I'm all the way in the middle of fucking nowhere. I have to drive ten hours back to Toronto tomorrow, and then you want to drive ten hours to New York? You're just getting overexcited because all your girlfriends are going. Think logically. Besides, you have reading to do, and remember, you don't even have a job yet."

My excitement had transformed into rage. Was he telling *me* to be logical? I was the logical one. He was usually the one telling me to relax and take things as they came. I couldn't believe that my lighthearted honey-bunny was acting like such an asshole. That was when I'd decided I was definitely going and had put the message on the chat.

So there I'd been, about to rush for the bus with only a couple of minutes to spare. I'd known that I had to make that phone call, and I'd known I wouldn't want to do it on the bus, with people around listening in. He was going to be pissed. And I didn't have time for an argument, but I also couldn't travel to another country without telling him, could I?

I'd picked up my phone and looked at my contacts. I'd smiled and then started dialing my parents.

"Hi, Pa, it's me. Sorry to wake you."

"I'm awake," my father had answered groggily. I could tell he was lying. He had likely fallen asleep in bed while watching television. I could picture him snoring away peacefully, my mom's head on his shoulder.

"I'm calling because I'm leaving for New York City, and I thought I should tell someone."

I'd known how strange that had sounded. There had been silence on the other end as my dad had probably tried to absorb what I was saying, his eyes open but his mind asleep.

"Dad, I haven't told Sam because when I told him that I wanted to go on the annual law school trip, he didn't react well. I just got a last-minute ticket, and the bus is leaving in a few minutes. I have to go. I'll call you when I'm back."

"Okay, have a good time," he'd said, his voice warm and reassuring. "Don't worry about Samir. This is a school trip. There's no reason why you shouldn't go and enjoy yourself."

That's my father—always siding with me. I've always thought it's because he knows I think things through before acting, but my mom maintains that it's because I'm his little girl and he can't see past that.

"Pa, I gotta go. I'm back on Sunday. I'll call you then."

I'd hung up and run out the door, wheeling my suitcase that was far too large for a weekend trip along behind me.

2

I was so tired. So very, very tired. I just wanted to curl up and sleep. Which would have been almost okay if the steady snoring coming from the audience below was any indication. But we were seated in a side balcony, almost as on display as the actors on the stage, so there was no way I was going to nap during *Hamilton*. Besides, Stephanie had sacrificed most of her morning standing in line for the impossible-to-get tickets. That half bottle of wine at dinner had maybe been a mistake.

Soon the steady pressure on my bladder, rather than proper behavior, was the thing keeping me awake. Damn it, not again! This had been happening all day and all last night. I shuddered, remembering the horror of the toilet on the bus. Luckily, our seats were perfect for mid performance escapes, so I climbed over Steph and bolted for the tiny staircase leading to salvation.

"I've been thinking about your situation," Steph said later on the walk back to the hotel.

"What situation?"

"Well, you were feeling sick earlier, and you've made a ridiculous number of trips to the washroom, and you almost fell asleep during only the most amazing musical ever. Not to mention that you're late."

Ugh. I had said something about that earlier, when we were getting ready, but I hadn't really thought anyone had heard.

Wait a second..."Um, are you saying I should take a test?"

Steph grinned. "Actually, yeah. Sel, don't you think you should find out for sure?"

I sort of listened as she continued providing me with reasons of why I should take a pregnancy test. I couldn't believe this hadn't occurred to me, but all the signs were there, as she'd so helpfully pointed out. Still, it had been a long day, if you counted the bus ride from hell on top of the shopping and the walking and the wine. No wonder I was sick and tired.

By this point Jade had joined the conversation. "So are you gonna do it?"

"Okay," I replied, "but only for your entertainment. And not with you guys around—I'll get performance anxiety."

Jade rolled her eyes. "Fine. Just call us as soon as you know."

I ducked into a pharmacy near our hotel, and they continued, making me swear I'd tell them first before they left me. Inside, I found the narrow aisle that seemed to hold all things reproductive-related: condoms, pregnancy tests, and diapers. Odd combination.

The aisle was also filled with bins and boxes for restocking. Big gray bins completely obstructed my access to the top shelf, where the pregnancy tests were. I tried to shove them aside, but the stack was as tall as me, and I hadn't gone to the gym since my first year of law school.

Great. That meant I would need someone to help me with this thing I didn't want anyone to know about. I started trolling the aisles for an employee, but found no one but the overworked cashier. Instead, I came across Alex and Jane in the water aisle.

Well, Alex was tall, at least. But how could I ask her to do this for me? I suddenly felt so embarrassed. Who was this person, almost a lawyer, married to a great guy, who was buying a pregnancy test at midnight so far from home? That couldn't be me. Could I reveal that me to someone I barely knew?

But I had to know. The rest of the trip would be torture—self-inflicted, as well as from Steph and Jade—if I didn't determine once and for all that I wasn't pregnant.

Alex looked back at me, concerned. "Selena, are you all right? You have a strange expression on your face."

LAW GIRL'S BUMP IN THE ROAD

"Well," I responded, my stupid smile freezing in place, "I'm actually not all right. Can you come with me for a second, Alex?" I crossed my fingers, hoping Jane would find choosing the perfect water more important than whatever crisis I was having.

"Sure, Selena."

I led Alex to the aisle of reproductive horrors and showed her the bins. "I need what's above those bins."

She looked up, then looked back at me with a giddy smile on her face. She shoved another bin over, then stood on it to reach over the tower in front of the pregnancy tests and handed me the first one she could grab.

I looked at the box, which had a baby's picture on it and, in a large font, the number seven. "Um, I can't take this test. I think it's for a couple who is trying to get pregnant."

She took the box from me and we both giggled. It was for people in a different situation than me. I also couldn't handle the baby's picture on the box. Sure, it was a cute baby, but the thought of a baby in my life at this point made me cringe with fear—and a little bit of disgust. The wall of diapers surrounding us didn't help.

Alex stepped up on the bin again and reached for another test. I looked at it, wondering how much money I would have to waste on the stupid thing. If only I could see the other tests so that I could get the cheapest one. But I didn't dare ask poor Alex for any more favors at this point—except one.

"Could you maybe distract Jane while I buy this? I don't really want people to know."

"Of course, Selena. I won't tell."

"Thanks."

I placed the test on the counter in front of the cashier, acting like it was no big deal. After studying the box for way more time than was necessary, the young guy finally rang it up and said, "That will be fifteen dollars, please." I guess it wasn't as much as it could have been. Not that I had any idea how much these things were supposed to cost. The only times I'd ever encountered them were in movies, when the characters always seemed to buy dozens of them, as if any more than one or two would change the diagnosis. Now at least I knew how much they were hypothetically spending on those dozens of tests.

Back at our room, I flung my gloves and coat on a chair and bolted for the bathroom, locking the door behind me. I laid out my purchase on the vanity and tried to read the instructions, but my eyes kept skipping words and lines, perhaps because there was still a bit of alcohol in my system.

"Okay, I'm just going to do it." If I said it out loud, I had to do it.

I sat on the toilet and started to pee on the stick, staring at the empty window on it as I did.

Oh, my God! I hadn't even finished peeing, and a pink line was already appearing in the window. This couldn't be happening. Maybe one line meant not pregnant and two lines meant pregnant? I mean, I hadn't even read the instructions.

I flushed the toilet and rushed out of the bathroom.

"Alex, can you come in here for a second?" Jane glanced up from her phone only briefly. I pulled Alex inside, feeling mildly guilty for touching her with my unwashed hands.

I shoved the instructions at her. "Can you tell me what this means?"

Alex had had at least as much to drink as me, but clearly, she was handling it much better—maybe because of her height or the fact that she wasn't freaking out like I was. After only a few seconds and a glance at the stick, she announced, "You're pregnant!"

3

Pundits bickered on TV. Clothing rustled as Alex carefully folded the day's outfit and set out the next. Jane's thumbs tapped steadily at her phone, her face eerily beautiful in the glow of the screen. And I was pregnant.

Pregnant? I smiled, then giggled, then broke into hysterical laughter, but I shut it down when Jane looked up, her expression unreadable. She quickly resumed her texting, but I felt chastened and uncomfortable. This moment, right now, would be one of the most important in my life, but I was spending it surrounded by strangers. I changed into my pj's and got into bed without saying a word.

I just wanted to sleep. But one thought kept bothering me as I tossed in the bed. What was I going to do?

LAW GIRL'S BUMP IN THE ROAD

I'd always wanted to be a lawyer, ever since I'd seen Reese Witherspoon in *Legally Blonde.* And I was so, so close. At this point I was reminding myself of that on a daily basis: You're almost finished your seventh and final year of university. Just a couple of months left. You can do it.

As I'm sure most students in their final year of law school could tell you, the first four years of undergrad go by extremely fast. I'd known then that I couldn't happily enter the real world to sit in a cubicle with finance nerds for the rest of my life. The more enticing alternative was to attend grad school. The choice certainly wasn't difficult. I'd graduated with degrees in economics and finance from an American university, but, post-9/11, as a half-Indian girl, I wasn't the best candidate for a job in many people's eyes, or at least not for a job I wanted. Even if I did find some company to hire me, it was unlikely that I would get a work permit to stay in the United States—particularly since, at five-foot-four, I seemed to pose such a threat to society. If I ever had any doubts about my status as a potential terrorist, they were shot down almost every time I crossed the border. I was always the person chosen for the "random" check. My suitcases were the ones that were searched, my underwear often arriving in the greatest disarray.

With all this, it was a relatively easy choice to return to Canada and apply to law school. Canada was home, my safe haven, and law was my childhood dream. My parents weren't so convinced about my decision at first. Although my father had always viewed me as basically a flawless human being, his response when I'd announced as a child that I was going to become a lawyer was, "Lawyers are a dime a dozen!" My father had been educated as an accountant and was now an entrepreneur, so he had an extremely negative view of those "overcharging bottom-feeders." My mother had also indicated her dismay. "Lawyers have to stay in a library all day and read. Don't you think that sounds so boring?" Perhaps my mother's viewpoint was slightly more accurate than my father's, but by the time I entered law school, they had changed their opinion of lawyers and were ecstatic about my choice of profession—probably because they thought I'd handle all their legal issues. I wasn't about to burst their bubble.

Now all that seemed pointless. Sure, I had time to finish school and even the bar exam, but then what? I couldn't start a job just to go on mat leave a week later. And if I didn't start work right away, how much harder would it be to find a job a year later?

I groaned, and Jane and Alex exchanged glances. Jane asked, "Selena, are you okay?"

"Everything's fantastic. Just tired. Why do you ask?" There was no way Jane was going to know that my life was on the brink of falling apart.

Alex sat beside me on the bed. "Is there anything I can do to help you? Anyone we should call?" she whispered.

Ugh. Probably. I hadn't even thought of Sam yet. Now it was confirmed that I was the ditzy girl, I was the kid, and

Alex was playing mom to me—exactly the thing I'd never wanted to happen.

"No," I mumbled, rolling over and burrowing into the blankets. "I just want to sleep." She got the hint and patted my shoulder before getting up.

But I couldn't sleep. Now all I could think about was what telling Sam would be like. Sam and I had an interesting relationship. We'd lived together for a couple of years before I'd gone to law school. Now we were living in two different cities, and in the meantime, we had gotten married. We were only a couple of hours apart, so I saw him all the time, but it always felt like we were moving backward. In a couple more months we'd be under the same roof again, but before long it wouldn't be just us anymore: it would be us and a baby, whom we were not at all prepared for. We would only just have adjusted to living together again before this huge change happened.

I wasn't exactly looking forward to living with him again either. Having my own space had been kind of great. Don't get me wrong; living with him was so much fun, but therein lay the problem. We were like two kids when we were together. Everyone envied our close and fun relationship and our continual loving banter, but we never got anything done when we were together, and I was starting to see that as a potential problem. That was the main reason I'd maturely decided that attending university away from him and the big city was necessary. Of course, my mother-in-law thought it was unnatural and loathed our living situation, but I was used to that. She'd hated the fact that we'd lived together before marriage, and now she hated the fact that we didn't live together after marriage. Some people would never be happy!

Although I was pretty sure she'd be happy about the baby. If there's one thing mothers-in-law love, it's a grandchild. If I kept it. If I didn't, she could never know. Which was why I wasn't ready to tell Sam.

Besides, it was late. He had no idea I'd even gone to New York, and now, past midnight, wasn't the time to drop that bomb, never mind the baby one.

I opened my eyes the next morning and a clear thought came to my mind: I'm keeping it. I was actually pregnant, and I was going to have a little life to care for.

I was at peace with my decision. I had been a little confused, to say the least, the night before, but now I was clear—although slightly hungover.

I looked over to see Aisha just waking beside me. She must have come in quite late.

"Morning, Aisha. How was your evening?"

"It was good. We went to an amazing Italian restaurant. It was a cute little place right down the street, and the food was delicious." Aisha continued telling me about what she'd eaten, and my stomach growled.

Aisha giggled, then asked, "Didn't you guys go somewhere cool last night? And you're hungry already?"

Oh, God. "I have to tell you something, but you can't tell anyone. I mean, I don't even know that what I'm going to tell you is true." I wasn't sure why I was telling her, but I just had to tell someone now that my decision was clear, and there was something about Aisha that made me want to tell her. We weren't close, but she was so sweet. Even though I was rambling, and I'm sure she desperately wanted to know what the hell I was talking about, she didn't pry. Instead, she waited for me to tell her my news.

"Aisha...Well, last night was interesting." This was the first time I was announcing the news to someone, and I wasn't really sure how to phrase it appropriately. So I just blurted it out. "I found out that I'm pregnant."

Aisha's reaction caught me completely off-guard. She jumped out of the covers and threw her arms around me. I flinched and glanced nervously at the sleeping women in the other bed.

"That's wonderful news!" she whispered excitedly.

Was it wonderful news? Did it warrant such excitement? I guess it did.

I stared at her, not sure how to react. I guess my confusion was obvious.

"Oh, Selena, I feel so insensitive. You are happy about the news, aren't you?"

"Well, to tell you the truth, last night I was a little shocked. Actually, I was totally nervous. I wasn't sure what I was going to do. But when I woke up, I knew immediately that I was going to have this baby. I mean, why wouldn't I have it? I'll be twenty-five next month, I'm married, Sam has a secure income, I'll have completed law school and the bar exams. I'll have the baby right before I actually start working as a lawyer."

Although I tried to sound confident, I realized that perhaps I was trying to convince myself of it too. But Aisha agreed with me.

"Selena, you are so lucky."

4

I had to tell Stephanie. I had to find her, and I had to find her now. And Sam, obviously, but Steph first, since she was close by. I searched for my phone so I could text her to meet me for breakfast, but it wasn't in my purse.

"Oh, shit," I muttered. I tried to remember when I'd used it last. I'd had it yesterday while shopping, but then what? I'd turned it off at the theater. Had it slipped between the seats instead of going into my purse? It must have. Oh, shit.

I picked up the room phone and dialed Steph, telling her to meet me in the hotel restaurant. Then I showered and bolted out the door.

In the restaurant I picked up a newspaper, but when the waiter came, I realized that I'd been staring at the front page without reading it at all.

"Um, just coffee for now, thanks."

He dashed off, and I began to panic. Was I allowed to drink coffee now? I couldn't be expected to cut it out cold, could I? I needed that morning cup, or I couldn't even function. And should I have ordered food? Was I starving my unborn child? There was so much I didn't know, and I couldn't even Google it.

I couldn't believe how worried I already was about this little thing I was carrying inside me. I felt like I was hiding a big secret, one that I had to care for immensely. On the other hand, maybe I wasn't even pregnant at all. Maybe I was just overreacting.

"Hope you haven't been waiting too long," Steph said as she sat down across from me. She started to look through the menu. "So, everything went all right last night?" she asked from behind it.

I smiled nervously. "No."

Steph looked up, her eyes wide, which thoroughly amused me. Just as she opened her mouth to say something, Catherine and Ethan walked up to our table. Ethan was wearing a suit. Who wears a suit to go sightseeing? Only Ethan, who had taken his future role as stuffy, proper lawyer to heart. Catherine, who'd grown up with people just like Ethan, seemed to be under the illusion that behavior like this was perfectly normal.

"Good morning, ladies," Ethan said.

"Care to join us?" I asked. I was enjoying making Steph suffer.

"Thanks, but New York is waiting. We're going to get started right away," Catherine answered.

They were about to leave, but Ethan paused. "Selena, last night at dinner I thought I overheard you saying something about a divorce. Did I hear you correctly?"

Oh God, I'd forgotten about that comment. Must have been the wine.

I laughed. "I was just joking that Sam may want a divorce because I didn't tell him I was going on this trip."

"What do you mean? He doesn't know you're here?"

I liked Ethan well enough, but sometimes he could be nosy. I knew if I let him, he'd keep asking questions. I had too much on my mind to play this game, so I had to shut him down.

"Yes, Ethan, that's exactly what I'm saying," I said abruptly, and I took a sip of coffee, glaring at him over the cup.

He took the hint. "I'm sure everything will work out." Then he looked at Catherine and asked her if she was ready to leave. Of course she was. She'd been ready from the moment they'd walked over to our table.

They finally left, and Steph turned back to me. She tried to resume the same piercing stare she'd had, waiting for me to offer something, but failed miserably and gave in first, giggling.

"So, Sel, what did you mean before?"

"Exactly what I said. No, everything did not turn out fine."

Before the conversation could continue, Jade came up to us. "What's so funny?" she asked.

I smiled, ready to get this over with. "I think you should sit down before I answer that."

"Okaaay," Jade replied.

Steph's face turned more serious, perhaps because she realized I wasn't joking. "Sel's saying that everything did not go okay last night."

"What are you guys talking about? Did I miss something?" asked Jade, completely confused.

"Remember I took a test last night?" I couldn't stop this stupid grin from appearing, perhaps because I didn't really know how to tell them the news. "Well, it changed color, or added a line, or whatever it's supposed to do, you know, when…"

Jade grabbed my wrist and whispered, "You're pregnant?"

I couldn't say a word. The stupid grin remained plastered on my face.

Steph jumped up and reached across the table, trying to wrap her arms around me. Instead, she fell, spilling my coffee and planting an elbow in a dish of jam. Jade and I jumped back like the seasoned pros we were to avoid the splash of coffee. We helped Steph up and wrapped her in a group hug.

"Oh my God, congratulations, Sel. This is so exciting!" Steph sobbed.

I felt my eyes welling up with tears, although I wasn't quite sure why. I looked at Jade and noticed that there were tears streaming down her face, ruining her perfectly applied makeup. I had never experienced this before. I was overwhelmed with emotion, and apparently so were my closest friends.

"You guys, why are we all crying? This is so ridiculous." We laughed and shuffled away from the table as servers came to clean up Steph's mess.

Jade dabbed at her face with a napkin. "So, what did Sam say, anyway?"

That stopped my laughing.

"Um, I haven't told him yet."

"What?" the two of them shrieked at once.

"It was late!" I explained. "I couldn't call him in the middle of the night. Especially since he doesn't even know I'm here."

Steph and Jade gave me significant looks. Not judging—just reminding me that, yep, those were just excuses.

"And I lost my phone."

Jade gasped. "You did? Any idea where?"

"I think it was in the theater."

"Don't worry. We'll call the theater, we'll get your phone back, you'll tell Sam, and everything will be amazing."

Of course it would. Of course I would tell him today, but of course I was nervous about it. By now he must have realized that I was in New York, which meant that he'd be furious with me—probably even more so if he'd tried to call my phone and I hadn't picked up. How would I tell him the news if he was just yelling at me? I knew, though, that I had to suck it up. I couldn't bear the idea of knowing something so major, something that would change both our lives forever, while he had no clue.

Steph smiled at us as she dabbed at the jam stain on her sweater. "I know. Let's go shopping. Then you'll be ready to tell him."

5

I'd always liked Sephora. The stores were so inviting—the scents that filled the air, the gemlike colors of makeup, the beautiful women who rushed up to you and solved all your problems. But as Steph and Jade were pulled in separate directions by helpful cosmetic angels, I wandered aimlessly around the store, my mind returning to worrying about Sam—and wondering how I'd call him, with my phone so far away. Jade had tried phoning the theater, but it wouldn't be open for hours.

I looked out the front window, scanning the street for a newspaper stand that sold phone cards. Outside it was dark and dismal, unbearably cold, and already I felt so tired. Was this something that happened to pregnant women? Oh, God, was I actually thinking of myself as a pregnant person? I had to call him. I had to tell him.

I was about to start looking for the girls so I could tell them I'd be back in a few minutes when I realized there was something I did need from Sephora. If I seriously was pregnant, I needed to think about how I would avoid stretch marks. I'd feared pregnancy my entire life because of the possibility of stretch marks. Sure, that seemed vain, but my mom's stomach was covered in terrible zigzaggy lines, and she was pale. On me, they'd stand out like tiger stripes. No more bikinis, no more crop tops at the gym—that's what I believed. And if there was a product out there that could genuinely help me to avoid stretch marks, this place should have it. It had everything. I needed someone to help me.

"Excuse me." I stopped a young woman in a black uniform. "I was wondering if you could help me."

"Of course. What can I help you with?"

What *could* she help me with? Should I say I'm pregnant? How could I tell this complete stranger before I even told my husband?

I smiled, feeling foolish. I wasn't even showing or anything, so she'd probably think I was being superparanoid.

"Do you have a product that will help me avoid getting stretch marks?"

"We have a few." I followed her to the back wall, and she pulled a jar off the shelf. "This one is for pregnant women. Is that what you need?"

I was relieved at how easy she made it. I actually felt comfortable talking to her.

"Yes, I'm really afraid of getting them."

"You're pregnant?" she asked in an enthusiastic voice.

"Yes," I responded, mine not so enthusiastic.

"Oh, that's so exciting," she said, bursting with excitement. "I want to have a child so badly, but my husband has a young child from his previous marriage and isn't ready for another." The woman continued talking, which confused me a bit. Why was she telling me her life story? It made me feel bad for her and guilty about my own feelings. Here was a woman who longed to carry a child. Meanwhile, I was worried about stretch marks, and I hadn't even told my husband about the pregnancy.

Jade suddenly appeared, interrupting the woman's tale. Without waiting for my response, she grabbed the product out of my hand.

"Selena, please don't tell me you're actually going to buy this."

I couldn't. I needed to talk to Sam before all this pregnancy stuff would seem real. Buying stretch-mark cream felt foolish.

After I picked up a phone card, we hopped in a cab and headed for the MOMA, arriving to find a massive lineup of people. Outside, it was bitterly cold.

Stephanie huddled close to me and whispered, "How badly do we really want to go to the art gallery?"

I giggled; I knew she was whispering so Jade wouldn't hear. Jade really wanted to go to the gallery, and if she heard us, she'd accuse us of acting prissy. So Steph and I amused ourselves by going to ridiculous lengths to keep warm, putting our hands in each other's pockets and seeing who could jump higher. Steph lit a cigarette, joking that we could warm our hands over the glowing tip.

I gawked at her. "Steph, you're killing my unborn baby!" I cried, mostly teasingly.

"Dammit! Remind me to never have children. I'll probably forget them in the car or something."

We finally reached the doors...only to see that the line continued inside. At least inside the heating was cranked up.

Once we had our tickets, we decided on a meeting time and place in case we got separated, which was bound to happen because it was already late afternoon and I had yet to phone Sam. I still wasn't sure how I was going to tell him. I guessed it would depend on his mood, which I expected would not be good at this point, given that this was the second day I hadn't talked to him.

As we walked through the contemporary art exhibit, I could no longer focus on the art. Usually it amused me—was I supposed to be impressed by it? Just because it's in a gallery, does that make it art? I stood in front of a plain canvas splashed with red paint and wondered how much it was worth. Probably more than I could even imagine, although I would never understand why. And then I realized that soon something quite similar would be hanging on my fridge. I guessed I'd better start appreciating it.

It's hard to motivate yourself to call someone when you know he's going to be furious with you. But I still had thirty minutes before my meeting time with the girls, so I decided to stop procrastinating and find a public phone.

Luckily, the pay phones were by the washrooms, because I really had to use the washroom. Or was I still procrastinating? Nope; as I got closer, I realized that I did in fact need to go. Already it seemed like I always needed to go.

Yet another lineup. I took the washroom lineup opportunity to plan my conversation with Sam. What tone should I use? Should I sound excited that I was in New York? No, that would only anger him more. I guessed I could sound apologetic, but that would only make him believe that the manner in which he'd spoken to me was acceptable, and it certainly was not. I'd left without telling him specifically because of the things he'd said and the way he'd said them.

A stall finally freed up. As I left it and walked up to the sink, my eyes fixed upon a woman holding a little baby. I guessed it was only a few months old, although I wasn't sure exactly. I hadn't been around many babies.

She was holding it really close to her chest. As I got closer, I noticed that she was breastfeeding. Her sweater was pulled up, and both boobs were hanging out for everyone to see. Oh my God, this woman was breastfeeding in public! Well, in a public bathroom, at least. Was this normal? Had I seen this before? Maybe this happened all the time and I'd just never noticed.

The woman looked up, and her eyes met mine. Usually when a woman catches you staring, she'll glare back at you as if to say, "What the hell are you looking at?" But this bare-breasted woman looked at me proudly as if she was saying, "Isn't my baby adorable? I don't blame you for looking."

I was superuncomfortable. I felt as if I were alone in the bathroom with this saggy-boobed breastfeeding woman, but there were so many other people there, so I didn't know what my problem was. If I weren't pregnant, I don't think it would have affected me at all. But the fact that in a year I could be that woman had rattled me. It was just starting to dawn on me how numerous and radical were the ways in which this baby would change my life. I quickly dried my hands and walked out as fast as I could.

Unbelievably, I had to stand in line for a phone too. How could there be so many people in one place without cell phones? As I stood there, my mind drifted to the bathroom woman. She was so much older than me—she must have been in her late thirties. I felt like a kid beside her. She'd seemed so proud to be a mom, and it had looked like she knew exactly what she was doing. She was proud and happy, and I couldn't imagine being the same in her situation: being out in public with my boobs hanging out, stretch marks on display, no makeup, and disheveled hair.

How could I do this? I couldn't be pregnant; I was too young. Even if I was pregnant, I couldn't possibly provide a child with the support it needed. I was more responsible than most women my age, but Sam and I were such kids. How could we take care of a kid? He wouldn't want the responsibility. We'd both agreed that we wanted children, but that was supposed to be in a few years. How could I tell him that our entire life plan needed to be altered?

It was finally my turn. As the phone rang, my anxiety began to increase. Well, there was no turning back now.

6

"Hello?" said my husband's voice.

"Hi, Sam," I said pleasantly.

"Oh, you decided to call." I could tell he was pissed. "I was worried sick about you. Who the hell do you think you are, going to New York without even telling me? I called your parents looking for you because I was worried when I hadn't heard from you. So you and your parents have this whole conspiracy thing worked out quite well. I guess now that I've heard your voice and know you're alive, I'll talk to you later."

I heard a click.

Dumbfounded, I gently put the receiver back on the phone. As I turned from the phone, I spotted a seating area, so I walked over to the black leather chairs and plopped down in one of them.

What had just happened? That conversation hadn't gone at all how I'd anticipated, and I'd thought I'd anticipated the worst. I hadn't even been able to tell him anything. Sam and I fought often, but this was different. Now he was also upset at my parents. We'd never conspired against him! What had my parents said to him?

I looked at my watch and noticed that I still had time before I had to meet the girls, so I decided to go back to the phones and call my parents. They might be able to shed some light on the situation that I was now faced with.

My mom answered on the third ring.

"Ma, it's me."

"How's New York?" she asked in her usual overly cheerful voice.

"It's good, but I just talked to Sam...Well, I didn't really get to talk to him, but I called him," I muttered.

"Oh, he called us really late last night."

"Yeah, I figured that part out. What did you say?"

"I didn't hear the phone because I was fast asleep, but your dad was only partially asleep. You know, when he dozes off during a movie and then wakes up over and over again until he finally switches the television off—"

"Ma, just tell me what happened. I'm using a phone card and it's going to run out soon."

"Okay, calm down. Jeez." That was so like my mother, a complete drama queen. Now she was acting like I'd insulted her by cutting her off when all she was doing was rambling to begin with.

"Ma, please tell me what happened!" I begged in as polite a tone as I could.

"Your dad was half asleep but awake enough that he heard the phone. Samir said he was worried about you, and your dad said that you were fine and not to worry. Then your dad said bye."

"That's it. That's all that happened?"

"Well, yeah. You know how your dad is when he's drowsy. He was sort of abrupt. Why? What did Samir tell you?"

"He was saying something ridiculous about a conspiracy."

"Well, Selena, we weren't quite sure if we should tell him where you were, but regardless of that, Samir didn't ask, so we didn't volunteer it. At least that is what your dad said to me this morning."

I loved the way my parents always projected a united front to the outside world. My mom hadn't even been awake at the time, but she had no problem claiming that "we" weren't sure whether to tell him.

"Ma, you didn't say anything wrong. If he calls again, which I doubt he will, then feel free to tell him whatever. It was not my intention to hide anything from him; it's just that I didn't want to tell him that I was going when I left because he was being so difficult."

A voice broke in and said, "You have one minute remaining."

"Ma, I gotta go, the phone card is going to run out. I'll talk to you later."

"Have fun in New York! I love you, darling."

"You too. Bye."

I've always had difficulty telling people that I love them, particularly on the phone. I wondered if she'd noticed. Of course she had—my mother noticed everything.

I walked back to the leather chairs, only to find that there was no longer any space available. Really, there was a line for the chairs now? I looked at my watch and noticed it was time to meet the girls, so I went to our meeting spot and waited. I mean, I wasn't with the most punctual people.

As I waited for my friends, an indescribable sadness came over me. Here I was in New York, on what was supposed to be a fun trip with my girlfriends, but instead I was feeling lonely. I just wanted Sam to hug me and tell me everything was going to be okay.

Until now my husband had always had a glass-half-full personality. Even when it didn't make sense to be positive, he'd never viewed anything in a negative light. But I couldn't imagine him doing so with the news I still had to give him. I couldn't imagine him being able to hold me and tell me what I wanted so desperately to hear from him.

— —

It was inevitable that the bus ride home was going to be a long one. It would lend me too much time to think about my situation and how I was going to deal with it. I'd decided to pick up a piled-high smoked-meat sandwich from the deli next door to the hotel. I had to start eating healthier, meaning a complete overhaul of my current diet—which included the sixth food group, junk food, as a staple—was in order. Soon. I wanted a healthy baby, naturally, so I at least had to try my best to ensure that outcome.

I closed my eyes and curled into my bus seat in an attempt to sleep, but I really wasn't tired, and the anxiety caused by my situation was becoming increasingly unbearable. I needed this time to sort out my next move. For my entire life, I had created plans and then executed them, so I was overwhelmed by this interruption. For the first time a plan had been executed for me without my doing. Okay, well, with my doing, of course, but without my intention.

I started to think about when and how this could have happened. I'd gone to Vancouver with my mom during the Christmas holidays. I'd left Toronto on December twenty-first and returned on January third. Sam and I had been together for one night before I left for Kingston, but I couldn't remember whether anything had happened. I'd been so tired from my trip, and I'd had to unpack and immediately repack to leave again. I'd returned home again the next weekend, which was the second weekend in January. The third weekend I was home again, but Sam had been in Florida for a business convention. The fourth weekend I was in New York...

Wait a minute; that meant I had been pregnant for only two weeks. That wasn't possible. I knew the test I'd taken had said "Early Pregnancy Test" on the package, but come on, this was really early! If only I could remember how late I was. Ever since I'd been on the pill, I'd stopped monitoring the dates.

Wait, I'd been on the pill! Except...I hadn't. I'd booked my flight to Vancouver a few hours before it had been scheduled to leave because I'd decided at the last minute to attend my great-uncle's funeral with my mom. I'd had no other plans for the holidays, so I'd decided to visit family and friends while I could. Sam had agreed it was a good idea, so when I'd bought the ticket, I'd called him and told him that I'd need a ride to the airport in an hour and a half.

"You booked your ticket? You're actually going somewhere without me?"

"You told me I should go and spend time with my family!"

"Yeah, but I was just being polite. I never thought you would actually do it."

LEIA LONDON

It was at that moment that I'd realized he was really upset with me. But there was little he could do without sounding like a complete jerk. We both knew that I was going for the vacation more than the funeral of my ninety-five-year-old great uncle whom I barely knew, but neither of us could say that out loud. The tension between us had been immense.

After I'd got off the phone, I'd started packing, trying to ignore the stress. But as carefully as I'd planned everything, I'd managed to arrive in Vancouver without my pills.

Despite the manner in which I'd left, my trip was fantastic. I mean, the funeral part hadn't been so fantastic, but the time with my cousins, my aunts, and my mom had been great. We'd spent a lot of late nights giggling over the stories my mom and her sister told about their childhood, the mischief they'd gotten into that of course they'd denied my entire life and apparently felt that I was now old enough to be privy to. They told me about the time my mom had left the house for a date with my dad wearing a miniskirt under her long skirt. After their date, she'd thought she'd have time to change at home before my grandfather got there, but he drove past her on the way home and caught her bare-kneed. I'd never seen her wear anything close to short, so the idea of her in a miniskirt blew my mind.

The time I'd spent with my family had been so much fun, in fact, that I'd completely forgotten to pick up some pills in Vancouver. By the time I'd gotten home, the habit had been broken.

I stared out the window of the bus as it continued to hum along the road, recalling my return from the Vancouver trip. I'd been in Toronto overnight before heading back to Kingston for my last semester of law school. Sam had been irritated that I'd been in such a hurry to return to school.

"You don't even have class tomorrow, so why are you leaving in such a hurry?"

"I've already explained this to you. I told you that I need to be on campus to change my courses before classes start."

"Why can't you just do it online?"

"Because if they let us do that, all of us would change our courses all the time."

"Yeah, like you. You're the one who chose your classes, so just deal with it."

It had seemed like everything I did caused a debate. He was starting to act as if he thought I should be fulfilling my duties as his wife, whatever they were. I'd maintained when we got married that my education came first, and at the time he'd seemed to understand, but something had changed in the year and a half since then.

Sam, like me, had been born and raised in Canada, but his home was a traditional Indian one. His parents had certain expectations of the role of a wife, and although he'd seemed to have a more modern opinion before we got married, that had been gradually changing ever since. My mom was Indian, but my father wasn't, so our home hadn't been traditional, and it was getting harder and harder for me to relate or to live up to Sam's changing expectations and attitudes on certain issues. For a marriage to be successful, there had to be compromise, but our willingness to compromise seemed to be decreasing. Still, I had only one semester left. After that, everything would return to normal, I'd assured him. And at the time I'd believed it. Now nothing would be normal again.

Next thing I knew, the bus arrived in Kingston. It was pitch black outside except for the bright white streetlights and the blue safety lights all over campus. I stretched my arms over my head, yawned loudly, and noticed my neck was sore.

Of course.

7

The PowerPoint slides flashed one after the other, accompanied by my professor's lecture. Or presumably so—it suddenly dawned on me that I hadn't heard a word of the lecture thus far, and there were still two and a half hours of arbitration class to go. Ugh. I was counting the number of Monday International Commercial Arbitration classes left before I never had to attend another three-hour lecture again. At least there'd be one fewer after this.

Why arbitrate anyway? I wanted to be in a courtroom, a litigator, like on *Suits*. Arbitration was less adversarial and less costly; the way of the future, according to my professor—but so, so boring to learn in a classroom.

All I could think about was whether I was really pregnant. So at the break I decided to make a quick visit to the university health center. I estimated that it would take about twenty minutes, so I left my laptop and books on my desk so that the professor wouldn't think I'd left class for the day. We may have been in our very last year of grad school, but he still took attendance.

I'd never been to the health center, so I hadn't anticipated that the walk across campus would take as long as it did. It was really tucked away, maybe so people who weren't all that sick wouldn't bother going. When I finally made it, I went up to the receptionist and asked, through the little holes in the plexiglass separating us, to see a doctor.

"Do you have an appointment?"

"No."

"Well, do you want to make one?"

As if I would walk all the way to this underfunded hole-in-the-wall to make an appointment for some time in the future. That's what a phone was for.

"I was actually hoping to see a doctor now."

"Is it a medical emergency?"

"Well, kind of. I mean, it's not life-or-death. It's just really important." My eyes began to well up with tears—another fabulous trend that was starting to become my new normal. I struggled to speak in a clear enough voice that the woman would hear me through the glass, but it was getting harder to do thanks to the knot that had formed in the back of my throat.

"Okay, dear," the receptionist responded with a kinder look, sensing my anxiety. Not that it was difficult to notice with my eyes threatening to spill tears. She took my name and student number and said she'd set up my file.

I waited at the desk for her to deal with the whole file situation. I looked up at the clock and saw that already this situation had taken twenty-five minutes. My gaze shifted to the bright paper signs on the nearby wall—a warning about the cancellation policy and a request that visitors use hand sanitizer beside a big plastic jug holding a mysterious green jelly. Ugh. That stuff would more likely be the cause of disease.

The woman reappeared at the window. "You now have a file!" she exclaimed, sliding it under the window, as if it were some type of privilege. "Place your file in the nurse's box. You'll see a doctor after a preliminary screening with the nurse."

I hoped that obtaining my file would be the longest part of the process. The place looked deserted, so I was sure I'd get out of there quickly. I walked down the hall she'd pointed out to me and paused, dumbfounded, as I turned the corner.

I was staring at a cramped waiting room. There were more people waiting to see the nurse than there were chairs, and the nurse's inbox was packed with files. Down a farther hallway I could see another waiting area crowded with people. I guess my look of shock combined with annoyance was obvious to the scrawny blond guy leaning against the wall for lack of anywhere else to go.

"It's always like this," he said in my direction. "It moves fast, though."

I smiled politely. Someone vacated a stained orange chair that had apparently been upholstered in the seventies, so I snagged it, trying not to think about how many diseased university kids had sat in that chair.

When had I become such a snob? Certainly not during my four years of undergrad, and I don't think it had been during my first two years of law school. I guessed I was finally ready to be done with school and get out into the real world. I felt a lot older than the undergrads sitting around me, I was tired of this small, quaint town, and I desperately wanted to return home to start life.

This was just great. I was missing my class, I had left my stuff behind, I had nothing to read, and my phone had no reception. I looked around at the people in the room. On my right was a guy reading his biology book and on my left was a girl wearing a mask. I doubted that the girl would humiliate herself by wearing the mask if she'd just had the common cold. No wonder someone had left this chair.

I picked up a *Cosmo* from a table. The magazine had mysterious stains on the cover that should have been coffee but weren't, but I was desperate to distract myself, so I flipped through it, eyeing the hot, young female bodies sporting the latest fashions. I was suddenly aware that my body was not going to look like that. I wouldn't be able to wear my clothes. A sudden rush of panic struck me. What would I wear? What about all the clothes I'd just bought at Century 21? How long was all that stuff going to fit me? I closed the magazine and tried desperately to think of happier thoughts to avoid the tears that were again forming in my eyes. Focus, Selena, focus on something, anything.

I looked around the room again. Everyone was extremely young. I'd bet that none of them were here for a pregnancy test. What would they say if they knew that's why I was here? But I was married and in my final year of school; I had a husband and a condo in downtown Toronto. I wasn't some punk kid just starting university. This was starting to become my mantra, the thing I had to tell people, or myself, to justify something perfectly normal. So why did I feel so uncomfortable about possibly being pregnant? I felt so young. Too young to have a kid. Too young to take care of another living being. I couldn't even take care of my stuff. My laptop was still in the classroom. My entire life was on that thing.

I walked back to the receptionist and asked, "Do you think I can leave for a few minutes? I'll be right back."

She stared at me as if I had offended her personally. Apparently, she was waiting for a better explanation.

"I left my laptop and books in my class because I didn't realize it would take this long."

Still nothing.

"So I guess I'll be about ten minutes," I tried explaining.

As I turned to walk out the door, the receptionist said firmly, "If you leave, you will lose your spot, which means that you will have to go to the end of the line."

I couldn't believe that this woman would seriously make me wait all over again. I had already waited an hour!

"Okay," I muttered. I walked back to my seat beside the masked girl. As I sat down, the chair tipped toward her and I shot back up, then mumbled an apology when I realized how rude that had probably seemed.

I had to pee anyway, so I stepped into the washroom, which was, not surprisingly, horrible and dated, with chipped tiles on the wall and a green stain in the sink where water had dripped from the taps for decades. At least it matched the general aura of the health center. Every bum that had touched the toilet I was about to use had belonged to a sick girl. I spent so much time wiping the toilet seat that I was almost too late.

I turned around to flush and noticed that my urine was cloudy. Was it always like this? Or was it the ancient toilet? I needed to Google this. And why was I staring at my pee? I was starting to become obsessed with my bodily functions. My behavior was starting to scare even me.

As I walked back to my chair yet again, a warm voice called my name. A pleasant lady was standing in the doorway. I followed the nurse into her little examining room.

"So what seems to be the problem?" she asked pleasantly.

"Well, I guess the problem is that I need to know if I'm pregnant."

"Oh," the nurse said, her casual, friendly manner turning to concern. "Well, that's not the cold that's going around, is it?"

"No, I guess it's not," I said awkwardly.

The nurse picked up her pen. "When was the first day of your last period?"

"I know that it was just after Christmas sometime," I answered.

"You aren't sure?"

"Well, I stopped monitoring dates years ago because I've been on the pill."

"If you're on the pill, then there is a ninety-nine percent chance that you're not pregnant. It must be a false alarm." She acted as if she were consoling herself. She seemed really worried that I could be pregnant, which was making me feel extremely uncomfortable as I continued to sit in her office. "You scared me for a second. Not many women at this established educational institution come here with this prob...I mean complaint. That's not the right word. You know what I'm trying to say."

Wow, I was right. The nurse was more nervous than me about the possibility of me being pregnant. I put my left hand on the desk, hoping she would see the sparkling solitaire and accompanying band on my ring finger. Perhaps she was nervous because she thought I was some undergrad who'd gotten knocked up.

Just as I was about to set the record straight, she said, "You know, sometimes women have irregular periods. It's not uncommon, and there is no cause for concern. Just to confirm: you are on the birth control pill, right?"

"Usually, yes," I answered.

"What do you mean 'usually'?"

"I've been on the pill for some time now, but this past month and a bit I was off."

"You were off what?"

Did I have to spell everything out for this woman? "Off the pill."

"I see," said the nurse, somewhat disapprovingly, as she peered over her reading glasses at me. I couldn't believe she was judging me, although I couldn't blame her, I guess. I might have done the same if I was her, but I still didn't appreciate it, under the circumstances.

Before the nurse could get another word in, I said, "I'm a grad student, a law student. I'm married, and if I'm pregnant, then, well, it's no big deal." There I went again. Who was I trying to convince?

"Hmmm," she said. "No big deal," she repeated as she scribbled something on my chart.

Even better, I thought. She was probably going to call Children's Aid on my ass before I'd even given birth to this child. I had to fix this.

"I don't mean that it's no big deal, but rather that I will handle it. It will be okay."

"What about your husband? Will he be there to handle it, as you say?"

What was she asking? Of course he would be there. As I watched her, I realized that maybe she wondered if my husband would be scared off by the news. I continued to analyze her expression, trying to understand what she was actually saying.

"Will he be there to support you and the baby?" the nurse prodded.

I felt a knot forming in my throat. I didn't want to cry in front of this woman. I just wanted to know if I was pregnant. Why was she giving me the third degree?

In the most polite, calm voice I could muster, I gently asked, "Could we please just figure out if I'm pregnant instead of playing the what-if game?"

Finally she approved of something I'd said. "Certainly," she replied. She stood up and took a tiny plastic drinking cup from a cabinet and handed it to me. "Pee in this cup, and then we'll test it on the spot."

I walked down the hall to the washroom I'd just escaped from. Peeing these days was no problem, at least. I returned to the nurse's office, and with a gloved hand she took the cup from me and stuck a thin strip of paper in. This seemed even more archaic than the stick I'd peed on.

The nurse pulled the paper out of my pee cup and announced, "You're pregnant."

I stared at the nurse. This was the second time I'd heard this. It couldn't be a coincidence.

Now what? Did I just go back to class?

The nurse interrupted my thoughts. "It's time to see the doctor." She ushered me down the hall and straight into the doctor's office. The nurse whispered a few things to the doctor and then let herself out of the office, closing the door behind her.

Pregnancy certainly had its advantages at the university health center. At least I didn't have to wait in line to see the doctor.

The doctor looked me in the eye and said, "So, you're pregnant."

"Yes, apparently," I responded.

She smiled as if to reassure me that this was okay and asked, "Was this planned?"

"No," I responded. "It's fine, though. I'm married, I'm almost done with law school. Everything will be fine." I needed to find a way to stop explaining myself like this was a problem. And I was pretty sure that my "everything will be fine" statement didn't come out all that believable.

"Do you want to discuss options? Or do you want to come back another day to discuss the situation?" She was very sweet about tiptoeing around what she was trying to get at, but I certainly didn't want to talk about abortion, at least not right now and not with her.

"I needed to know if I was pregnant and I now know, so thank you for that. That's all I came here for, so I guess I'll head out now. I have a class to get back to, so...um, I guess I'll head back to it." I stood up as the doctor remained seated with her eyes fixed on mine. "I'm fine, really," I said, trying desperately to convince her. I said, "Thank you" and quickly let myself out.

I walked swiftly down the hall with my eye on the turn in the hallway. If I could make the turn without the doctor or nurse coming after me, I'd be home free. I was two steps away when I felt a tap on my shoulder.

"Dear," the pee-cup nurse said, "take this brochure and please call if you need anything."

I looked down at it. A pregnant woman, hand on belly, looked out a window. "You're not alone. You have options," was printed in Comic Sans on the window. It was for the local pregnancy crisis center. Oh geez, why did they think I needed this?

I looked at the nurse, gave her a half smile, and walked swiftly out of the health center. I could finally breathe. I tossed the stupid brochure into the first garbage can I saw on my walk back across campus.

My books and laptop were sitting in the lecture room, miraculously, abandoned an hour earlier by all the students whose eyes had likely glazed over from boredom in the International Commercial Arbitration class.

I returned to my apartment, where I collapsed on the sofa, my book bag still over my shoulder and my Pumas on my feet. My eyes had grown heavy, my body was aching, and it was as if my brain had shut off. I couldn't think about anything but sleep. I stared at the remote control that sat just out of reach on the coffee table, but I was too lazy to reach for it. This was ridiculous. It was only three-thirty in the afternoon.

But before I could take a nap, there was one thing I had to take care of, something that always motivated me to move. I had to make a list. I grabbed a pen and notebook from my bag, which at least was in reach.

1. Get someone's class notes from arbitration.
2. Make appointment with Dr. Robinson.
3. Get groceries—fruits, veggies, prenatal vitamins.
4. Buy pregnancy book!
5. Call Sam. This time for sure.

I knew there were other things I should jot down, but the list already seemed daunting.

I reached in my bag for my phone and scrolled for my family doctor's number.

"Hello. Doctor's office. How may I help you?" a young voice—not the usual cranky old woman—said through the phone.

"I need to make an appointment with Dr. Robinson."

"Okay, how's April twenty-seventh?"

"Do you mean February twenty-seventh?" I asked innocently.

"No, I mean April," the receptionist emphasized as if I were incompetent. Perhaps the crabby old lady was better than Little Miss Attitude.

"I need to see Dr. Robinson as soon as I can, and I was hoping for this Friday."

"Well, I don't see how that is possible," retorted the girl.

"Look," I said, getting frustrated. "I just found out that I'm pregnant, and I need to see her to discuss that."

"What about next Friday?"

"Listen, I need to see her this Friday. I live in Kingston—well, I mean, I live in Toronto, but I'm in Kingston right now, and I can only come into town this Thursday night and leave on Sunday because I'm in school here, law school." I realized after blurting out all that information that I sounded like a rambling idiot. "Why don't you ask Dr. Robinson if she can squeeze me in on Friday? I realize that she's busy, but I've been her patient for years, and I doubt she would mind, given the circumstances."

"Okay, hold one minute," said the woman. Then I heard silence. I wasn't sure if she had put me on hold or hung up on me. I felt my eyes growing heavy and weepy. This had to stop, this crying business. I had cried more during this pregnancy thing than I had since I was ten years old.

The woman came back on the phone and said, "I've booked you in for Friday at eleven a.m."

"Okay, thanks," I said meekly through the lump in my throat. I hung up, then grabbed my list and checked that off.

I took my shoes off and lay down, pulling the throw blanket over me. Tears started streaming down my face, and I started to cry, loudly. There was no way I was going to knock anything else off my list right now. Especially that last item.

8

I got on the train Thursday evening, my bag stuffed full of dirty clothes. Doing laundry in the clean, quiet privacy of my condo was a million times better than lugging it down to the basement in my apartment building, where I would need way too many quarters that I didn't have because I'd given them all to Starbucks.

I desperately wanted to catch up on reading, but my eyes were heavy, and if I let my mind drift, then I was welling up in tears. I wasn't really sure why. Maybe fear of what everyone was going to say—or, more likely, fear caused by the fact that I was the biggest planner ever and this baby, at this point in my life, was not in my plan. I was supposed to be an established corporate lawyer on the partnership track, with published articles and an amazing salary, by the time I had children. And I was supposed to have the support of my husband. This was supposed to be happy, welcome news, not news I was struggling to share with him.

I looked at my phone, which I happened to have been clutching in my hand since sitting down on the train. I put the pink highlighter I'd been holding in my other hand in the seam of my open book. I was going to do it. It was time.

"Hello?" he answered, as if he didn't know who was calling—but obviously knowing, since my name would have appeared on his screen.

"Hi," I said quietly, holding back tears.

"You finally surfaced. Apparently my wife is not a figment of my imagination."

"I'm on the train home for the weekend."

"Just like that? Don't you think we need to talk about your behavior?"

My sad thoughts turned angry. "What do you mean 'my behavior'?" I replied. "I went on the law school trip. Get over it."

"When you are ready to talk to me like a proper wife, call me."

Then there was silence. Had he seriously hung up on me again? Why was he reprimanding me like I was a child? It was like he was becoming more traditional, expecting me to conform to a certain role, and because clearly that wasn't going to happen, we kept clashing.

But I was in no mood to fight. I was tired, and I needed my husband's comfort right now. I decided to text him. I had wanted to tell Sam the pregnancy news in person, but I couldn't wait the entire three-hour train-plus-cab ride, which is why I'd decided the next best thing was to call him from the train. But clearly that plan had failed.

I had no choice; I needed him to know. Maybe a text was a good thing. Then he'd have time to digest the news before I walked in the door:

"I wanted to tell you in person or at least on the phone but you hung up on me. I'm pregnant. ☺"

I hit send and watched my screen, waiting for a reply, barely blinking. After five minutes had passed for what should have taken seconds, I decided to send another text:

"Um, are you going to say anything?"

Again I just stared at my phone. I could have distracted myself by scrolling through Insta or Facebook, but I just wanted to see his reply, hear from him, whatever. And then it happened:

"WTF?"

Admittedly, I hadn't known how Sam would react to the news, but even still, his response left me wondering. Was this a good WTF or a bad WTF? Should I send a smiley emoji or a sad emoji? Should I try calling him again?

As I sat wondering, he sent another text:

"Serious? If yes, what are we going to do about it?"

I realized I'd been hoping he would be superexcited, which would have made me feel superexcited and put my mind at ease about the future. I desperately needed him to say, "Don't worry, sweetie, this is great news. We'll figure things out. You will be a superstar lawyer despite the timing of this pregnancy, and you will have a beautiful baby on top of a successful career." Of course, that was not the response I'd received.

I sent another text:

"I don't know what you are doing about it, but I am keeping it."

Almost as soon as I hit send, the phone rang. There was no exchange of hellos this time.

"Why didn't you tell me?"

"What are you talking about? I just told you," I said.

"This is good, right?" I wasn't sure if he was trying to convince me or himself.

"I guess it's good. I don't know. I can't believe this happened. I thought accidents were bullshit until now."

When I opened the door of our condo and dropped my bag, I was glad I'd dealt with the news. Sam walked up to me with a huge smile on his face and held me, and that was all I needed. All the worrying, all the arguing, and all the what-ifs disappeared. We were going to be a family.

We were seated in the waiting area for what seemed like hours. Finally, Dr. Robinson opened the door and called my name.

"Right here," I responded as I stood up. As I started walking toward her, I realized that Sam was following me. I turned to him and said, "I need to talk to her alone first. You know, girl talk."

"Okay," Sam said. I could tell that he was hurt by my request, but I didn't care. I needed to talk to my doctor one-on-one. She had been my physician for thirteen years and had seen me grow into the person I was today. She would be able to give me advice as a woman and as my doctor, but that would happen only if we were alone.

Dr. Robinson motioned me into one of the rooms. I took a seat in a chair and she sat across from me, placing my file on the desk. She looked up at me and said, "So, Selena, what brings you by?"

I looked at her and blurted out flatly, "I'm pregnant."

"Oh," she answered. Dr. Robinson was always grounded, with a calm that suggested that everything was going to be okay regardless of what I was facing. It was exactly what I needed.

Instead of asking whether it was planned and why I didn't seem ecstatic, she said, "I have two questions. First, how do you know that you are pregnant, and second, if you are in fact pregnant, how do you feel about this?"

"I took a home pregnancy test, which came up positive, and then I went to the health center at school and took another test that confirmed the pregnancy. So I'm certain. I'm sure you've already figured out that this wasn't planned, and quite honestly, I have no idea how I feel.

Had I gotten pregnant before I was married, I would certainly consider terminating the pregnancy, but I'm married, and this baby will be born after I finish law—well, anyway, my personal beliefs require that I keep the baby." I looked right into her eyes after what felt like a confession, as if I was waiting for some form of approval.

"How does your husband feel about the pregnancy?"

"He's scared shitless!"

Dr. Robinson laughed. "I love how you're always so forthright, Selena."

"He's scared now, but that's his nature. He's always initially scared by change. He takes a little while to adjust to things, but once he has, he is unable to imagine his life without whatever has been introduced into it. I'm certain this will apply to the baby."

"You know, I hate to stereotype, but many men are like this, and it's good that you've realized a key formula at your age. One more question. What did your mother say?"

Dr. Robinson was also my mother's physician. She knew my mom was a total drama queen. She also knew that my mom had extremely high expectations of me, which did not include me having a baby before starting my career. Making matters worse was the fact that I was turning my mother into a grandmother, which I knew she would despise because it meant that I was aging her.

"I haven't told her yet. You know how my mother is."

"Many couples don't tell people until after about three months anyway, so don't worry. You still have time to figure out how to tell her."

The doctor said that we needed to start talking seriously about the pregnancy. I interrupted her and asked if Sam could join us. I knew how upset he would be if I didn't include him in the conversation.

After he'd joined us, the first thing she did was pull out a little cardboard wheel. Sam stared at it suspiciously. "What's that for?" he asked as the doctor tried to move the cheap spinner that appeared to be stuck.

"This will tell us the baby's due date."

"You mean the day that the baby will actually be born?" he asked in disbelief. I realized that he still hadn't grasped the fact that I was carrying a life inside me.

"Selena, when was the first day of your last period?" This question was becoming routine. Suddenly, everyone felt entitled to ask about my period. I really missed the days when my period had been a private matter.

"Usually I would know the exact date, but this time it's a bit different because I wasn't on the pill and I'm not used to keeping track."

"What is your best guess?"

"I've tried to think about it prior to today, and I think that it was December twentieth."

"That would make the baby due on September seventeenth."

"What do you mean by your 'best guess'? You have to know the exact date. This is our baby's birthday." I could hear panic in Sam's voice, and I'm certain Dr. Robinson heard it too, because she let out a little giggle.

"Sam," she said, "it's not an exact science. The baby will come when he or she is ready to come. The baby may come early or may come late, so even if Selena was certain of her date, it doesn't mean that this little paper wheel could give us a definite answer."

We stared at the wheel in Dr. Robinson's hand. It was as though she were holding a tarot card.

"Okay, let's move on," she continued. "We still have a lot of ground to cover. It's extremely important that we book you at a hospital ASAP or there won't be space for you."

Now it was my turn to freak out. "What do you mean there won't be space? Where would I have the baby—on the street?"

"You know how our health care system is, Selena. You have to get a jump on everyone else. Aside from that fact, you will be set up with an ob-gyn at the hospital. It's just the system."

"Okay, I'd like to have the baby at Sunnybrook because I've heard the doctors and nurses are excellent. Also, I was born there, and look how wonderfully I turned out," I said with a smile.

"That's the witty Selena I know," said Dr. Robinson.

Sam interrupted. "Selena, shouldn't we ask about the various hospitals that are available instead of just choosing what you think is best?"

Here we go, I thought. I'm a decisive individual who does my research ahead of time. I already knew the pros and cons of each choice, and that's why I knew which hospital I wanted to use. Sam, on the other hand, needed someone to do his homework for him. I hadn't bothered telling him about what I'd learned because he would still want to hear it from an expert, which would only anger me because it meant that he was dismissing my opinion. We could be at a grocery store buying mangoes, and Sam would have to go to the fruit guy and get a lesson on mangoes before he would let me make the purchase. The most frustrating thing was that he didn't even like mangoes! My girlfriends had told me that this was how he showed his love for me: by always wanting me to get the best of what I wanted.

"Sam," said Dr. Robinson, "Sunnybrook is renowned for having doctors and nurses that specialize in women's health and tend to their needs." He seemed irritated but acquiesced, at least for the time being. "We should discuss your diet, Selena. Have you started taking folic acid pills?"

"Yes."

"What type?" I told her, and she nodded. "You have to maintain a healthy diet for the sake of—"

Sam interrupted again. "Is that the right pill?"

"Yes, it's fine," Dr. Robinson responded.

"Well, how many pills should she be taking and how often?"

Dr. Robinson was about to answer when I cut in. "I'm not an idiot. I discussed the brands with the pharmacist before choosing. I then read the instructions, which indicated that I should take one pill per day. Do you have to make a big deal about everything?"

Sam stared at me and said firmly, "Selena, it's important that we get the correct information from a professional."

This was ridiculous. Any five-year-old could follow the instructions of a pharmacist. As my mouth opened to say unkind things to my husband, Dr. Robinson interjected and said, "Selena, Sam is just trying to show he cares." Then she looked at him and said, "You have to show a little confidence in Selena's choices. She is caring for this child twenty-four/seven, and there are times when you will have to trust that what she is doing is in the best interests of your child. Without trusting in her decisions, your relationship will suffer."

Dr. Robinson was right, about both of us. I was surprised by her calm tone. She had patience that I envied.

She continued going over everything we had to do. I was completely prepared for my meeting with her, so I didn't feel overwhelmed, but from the corner of my eye, I noticed that my husband was on the verge of a nervous breakdown. I clutched his hand and smiled, doing my best to reassure him that, between his concern and my confidence, we had this.

9

I stopped drinking coffee, resulting in a week of withdrawal, during which I couldn't concentrate on anything. I felt like I was in a state of sleep with my eyes open. By the end of month two, at the height of my nausea, there was no way in hell I could have kept down coffee anyway. The thought of it made me retch, just as almost anything did: eating, moving, and even breathing. Brushing my teeth gave me the worst anxiety. I'd stare at my toothbrush, desperately wanting to clean my teeth, but knowing well what would happen when I did: even with just a tiny bit of toothpaste on it, as soon as I stuck it in my mouth, I'd start to heave. I still needed some caffeine to make it through class, so I switched to tea, and I had toast every morning on my way to school for the sake of the baby's health, but that was as much as my stomach could handle. The best food to eat when I was hungover was carbs, so using that logic I tried eating spaghetti and tomato sauce one evening. It tasted so bitter, as if someone had poured lemon juice all over my pasta. I tried a second bite, but it tasted worse than the first. I wanted to eat but couldn't.

Somehow I still had to endure law school until April. How would I manage? I couldn't eat anything without feeling sick, I was always tired, and I couldn't work out my frustration at the gym because all I wanted to do was go home and sleep. And I couldn't tell anyone why I was so miserable, because we still hadn't told our parents.

Sam was the type who told everything to everyone. He was incapable of keeping a secret. I convinced him that my pregnancy was the one thing that he couldn't talk to anyone about, not even his parents. I told him that we needed to wait until after the third month because statistics showed that many couples lost the baby within the first three months, and it was a superstition that you're not supposed to disclose pregnancy news until after the third month. It was one topic that Sam actually agreed to stay mum about.

Around the end of the second month, though, Sam called me and said he could no longer keep quiet. His mom was suggesting that Sam buy a condo in Montreal and run their hotel there for the time being. He had said he didn't want to, but Sam never said no to his mother, so she was suspicious.

"Samir," she'd said, "there isn't enough work for you to do in Toronto. There is no reason for you to be here. Selena's in Kingston, so there is no difference whether you stay in Toronto or Montreal. It's an equal distance from either city."

But he knew that I needed to come to Toronto for doctor's appointments and to be with my family on the weekends, because that was home. He'd snapped at his mom and told her he didn't want to talk about it, but that had made her even more suspicious—Sam rarely snapped at his mother. So he asked me if we could please tell her.

"Okay, it's just about the third month, and my tummy has become pudgy, so I guess we can tell your mom."

"Great!" Sam said enthusiastically. "I'll get my mom to invite your parents over for dinner on Saturday night, and we'll announce it then."

"Announce it then? Are you kidding?" I said. "I can't tell my mother."

Sam burst out laughing. "What do you mean? When do you want to tell her?"

"Never!" I said firmly.

"Selena, you're not thinking rationally. You're eventually going to start showing. How do you plan on keeping this from her?"

"I know I have to tell her. I'm just not ready yet." I didn't want to discuss this, but I knew I needed to compromise.

I also needed to tell my parents sometime before the baby was born. "I'm going to get on the phone and gauge how my parents feel about becoming grandparents."

Easier said than done. As I sat on my sofa in my Kingston apartment with my feet up on the coffee table, I stared out the window and watched the rain come down. It was a gloomy, cold day outside, and I was happy to be in my sweats and in the cozy warmth of the indoors. I knew I couldn't keep it from my parents any longer without feeling guilty, but I also didn't have the guts to tell my mother, who inevitably would be disappointed with me for not following the plan.

It seemed that no matter how well I did, she was eternally disappointed with my life choices. I'd told her I wanted to study economics and finance, and she'd been devastated that I wasn't studying science. I'd told her I was going to law school, and she'd been disappointed that it wasn't med school. I'd told her I was getting married, and there had been a long list of reasons she was completely disappointed by the person I was marrying and the time in my life when I chose to get married. While I was a teenager living at home, she had wanted to send me to boarding school in Switzerland because in her opinion I was getting into trouble, talking to boys, and unlikely to achieve any acceptable level of success. There had been many fights in which my dad had played referee. He hadn't taken sides, but according to my mother, he'd always sided with me.

While I had been dealing with her disappointment, my brother had been her baby, her "good" son. He was a year younger than me but had skipped grade two because it had been too easy or something, which meant that we'd been in the same grade. That had completely sucked for me. He was quiet and liked nights at home playing video games, computer programing, and doing things with electronics that I never really understood. He didn't have to study at school, but just waltzed in and aced everything. To this day, I have no idea how we were born and raised by the same parents—we are so completely different.

As difficult as it was going to be to disappoint my mother yet again, I was never one to procrastinate. And I had a work-around. I dialed my dad's cell.

"Hi!" my dad answered in a happy voice. I immediately felt so excited, just hearing him on the other end. Sometimes I didn't realize how much I missed my parents until I heard their voices on the phone or saw them in person.

"Hi, Pa!"

"How's Kingston? Only a couple of months and you'll be home. You must be so excited to finally move back after almost seven years away."

My dad was not normally chatty, particularly on the phone, but since I'd left for school, he'd become quite the chatterbox when I called. I wanted to get this conversation over with and didn't feel like engaging him in small talk right now.

"Kingston's okay, but I called to tell you something."

"Is something wrong?"

"Sort of," I said. "Well, not wrong, it's just...I'm not really sure how to tell you this. Please don't be disappointed in me. I can't handle a lecture right now." I had never rambled like this in any conversation with my father in my entire life.

"What's wrong? Everything will be fine, but I need to know what the issue is so we can figure out how to resolve things."

I loved how my father was already trying to solve my problem without knowing what the actual problem was. I breathed in deeply and exhaled slowly as my father waited for me to talk.

"I'm pregnant."

There was a momentary silence and then a sort of giddy laughter for a few seconds before my father replied.

"Wow! I wasn't expecting that news. I thought you were going to tell me you failed a course or something."

"No, I didn't fail a course. I have never failed a course in my entire life!" I snapped at my dad.

"Can you blame me? Look at how you were acting when you called," my father replied as he continued giggling. "So, have you told your mom yet?" My father's laughter trailed off as he asked that question.

"No, I can't tell her, and I don't want you to say anything. I'll tell her in person."

"You know she considers an omission of important information to be a lie, and you know how she feels about lies, and you know how she feels when you or I are hiding something from her. She will view our colluding as an act of war against her."

"I know, but I'm just not ready. Wait, so you aren't upset?"

"No, not at all. You're old enough and married, so what is there to be upset about? Just tell me that you are finishing law school."

"Of course I'm finishing. I'm so close to it being over, and the baby isn't due until September anyway."

My dad listened as I told him these intimate baby details, which felt strange to say out loud. I hadn't talked about "the baby" with anyone other than Sam yet.

"Good, just make sure you graduate from law school, and everything else will fall into place. Now, when are you telling your mother?" My father did not want to deal with her wrath, so I understood why he was quick to return to that question.

"I'm spending the weekend in Toronto. I have a doctor's appointment on Friday, so I guess I could come over for dinner on Friday night."

"That's three days away. Don't make it longer. Every day you wait to tell her is going to make it worse for us both."

He was right.

"Don't worry—three days, and she will know the news."

I hung up with my dad after he congratulated me, and I sat in the silence of my apartment with only the sound of the rain coming down in the background. I felt a sense of relief that my dad knew and that he was happy to become a grandfather. One parent down, three to go.

10

I told Sam that we were having dinner at my parents' house. I hadn't told him that my dad knew I was pregnant because then he would think it was okay to tell the whole world, and I wasn't ready. I had to tell my mom first.

"I was hoping we would have dinner with my parents tonight," he replied.

I looked at him and didn't say anything. We seemed to always argue about which parents we would meet on which days. His parents thought I should be with them at every possible moment. His mother in particular had told me after we were married that I was now her daughter. I'd naïvely thought at the time that this was sweet. It hadn't taken long for me to realize that she was serious. I was supposed to sever ties with my family and only see them on occasion, when "permitted." I was supposed to move in with Sam's family and be the good daughter-in-law. I was supposed to attend every wedding, funeral, birth ceremony, family dinner, hotel opening, hotel convention, and family trip—and the list went on—with them and only them. If there was time, I could see my parents. This was the traditional Indian mentality, but I'd had no idea that Sam's family was this traditional until my wedding. It would have been nice to know beforehand! I guess it likely would not have made a difference, because it was the kind of situation that you had to experience to believe.

I decided I had to make an enticing argument from the beginning, since I had no energy to argue. Ever since I'd learned I was pregnant, I was always tired. At times, keeping my eyes open was a chore, and staying awake past eight at night had become an impossible task. If I tried to force myself, not only was I fighting sleep, but the next day I would wake up with a solid headache. Because I was pregnant, I refused to take any medication, so I would just be stuck with a headache the entire day until it was time to sleep again. Afternoon naps had become essential to get me through my boring law school reading.

I looked at Sam and said, in a sweeter voice than normal, "I thought we would have dinner at my parents' house tonight because I thought we could spend one day during the weekend with your parents and one day we could spend alone."

"Oh, my mom would love it if we spent the day at her place. How about we stay the night on Saturday?"

Why he was always pushing the envelope was beyond me. Wasn't the whole day enough? Did we have to spend the night at his parents' house also?

"Let's see how things go. I have to drive back to Kingston on Sunday evening."

"Okay," he replied. Mission accomplished! Dinner at my parents' house was on.

We arrived at my parents' place at six. I had a key to the house, but my parents only locked the door at night or if they were out. They liked having an open-door policy for family and close friends. Sam thought the open-door policy was odd. He felt we should ring the doorbell and wait until someone opened the door for us, which was ridiculous because my parents' home was my home, and it always would be, regardless of what my mother-in-law thought. I could see him sticking his finger out to ring the doorbell, so I rushed past him and just waltzed through the front door like I always did.

"Ma, Pa, we're home!" I yelled as soon as I was in. Versace, my white shih tzu that I'd gotten in high school and that my mother had inherited when I'd gone away, ran to the door to greet us. He was really old and mostly enjoyed cuddling up with my mom and being stroked and brushed, which she loved doing. He was jumping up and wagging his tail, desperately wanting me to pick him up, so I did. I was cuddling him when Sam grabbed my arm.

"You can't lift him up. You can't lift anything heavy up right now."

I realized what Sam was talking about, but was Versace too heavy at eighteen pounds? I wasn't sure what "too heavy" was for me. I put the dog down for the time being, and as soon as I did my dad appeared.

"Hi there!" he said as he came to hug both me and Sam. "We're so happy you're joining us for dinner. How was the drive from Kingston?" he asked me. He was always asking about "the drive." He was genuinely interested in people's experience with traffic. I had no idea why, but I indulged him.

"It took about two and a half hours, smooth sailing the whole way. Hit a little traffic at the tail end of the four-oh-one."

"Ah," my dad said as he led us to the kitchen. "Likely where they are widening the shoulder. It's been backing things up a lot. You're lucky it didn't delay you an extra half hour to forty-five minutes. Look who's here!" he announced.

My mom was in the kitchen cooking, with the housekeeper by her side to assist with her every request. I called Anna my mom's paid companion. After my brother and I grew up, we no longer required a nanny, and after we moved out, my parents no longer required a full-time housekeeper. I, therefore, thought "paid companion" was appropriate. Anna helped in the kitchen and kept the place clean, but she also sat and watched television with my mom when my mom didn't want to be alone, and she listened to her complain about extended family members, chiming in occasionally with commentary as needed.

My mom hadn't heard us enter over the hood fan that she always set to the highest speed. It sounded like a jet engine, and I wasn't even convinced it was doing much to vent the air. She said it circulated the air, and all the windows needed to be open, as well as the patio door, for the cooking smells to escape. I realized that some meals, particularly if she was frying or using the indoor grill, needed the fan and all the windows and the patio door open, but I disagreed that every meal required this treatment. Did pasta and sauce require extensive fan use and window opening? There was no point in trying to convince her otherwise. In addition, she had at least three heavy-duty scented oils and candles that would be put into use as soon as the meal was cooked, which I anticipated would occur any minute. Then there was the music that would play during dinner, always through the intercom so it could be heard throughout the house. The music was usually something instrumental, like jazz or Spanish guitar, and since it was competing with the fan, it would blare through the worn-out speakers, accompanied by a hiss, inducing headaches if it went on longer than half an hour.

My mom put her cheek to mine and kissed the air, then kissed Sam on both cheeks. My mom and I never hugged—I'm not sure why; we just never did. She said I never wanted to hug her when I was little, so we'd never gotten into the habit.

"I hope you are hungry!" she announced. She had made grilled chicken wings in a honey-garlic sauce, veggie spring rolls, beef stir-fry noodles, and basil chicken with vegetables and rice. It smelled amazing, and the presentation was impeccable. All the food was on pretty platters, decorated with vegetable garnishes. My mom was an amazing cook, and she loved to see people enjoying her food.

The formal dining table was set for dinner, and we all took our places. As I bit into the spring roll, I remembered the delicious taste of home cooking. After I'd eaten several spring rolls, my mom said, "Wow, you must have been hungry. I don't think I've ever seen you eat four spring rolls at one sitting. You'd better save some room for the main course."

My dad smiled as he looked at me. I smiled back. We were hiding a big secret from my mom, and we derived pleasure from our secret, but at the same time, we both feared the consequences once she learned that we'd been keeping it from her.

I put some rice and chicken on my plate, took a bite, and felt an immediate sense of pure pleasure. "The food is sooo good, Ma," I said with food still in my mouth, which obviously was kind of rude but was okay because I was paying a compliment to the chef. I ate my entire serving and then reached over to the noodle dish.

My mom smiled and said, "I know you're enjoying a home-cooked meal, but what's gotten into you? I've never seen you eat this much and this fast."

"Ma, I was really starving. For some reason, I can't seem to eat enough to fill the void."

I couldn't look over at my dad, or I knew we would both burst out laughing. I looked at my mom, and she looked back at me from across the table. The time had come. I finished the last bit of the noodle dish and then opened my mouth to speak, when suddenly my mom stood up and said, "What can I get everyone? Tea or coffee? We are having homemade apple crumble and vanilla ice cream for dessert."

My mom's apple crumble was a crowd pleaser. She always made extra crumble on top for me because I just loved it with vanilla ice cream. I wasn't quite sure what to do, though: tell her the news or wait until after dessert. I was ready now. It couldn't wait one minute longer.

"Ma, I need to tell you something."

"Well, of course, Sweets. Let me just get dessert out and tea served, and then we can all head to the living room and catch up."

"No, Ma, I need to talk to you now. Forget about dessert and tea for a few minutes."

My mom's smile faded quickly. She did not like having her gourmet meal interrupted. She liked a perfect flow from one course to the next until all our bellies were sufficiently stuffed so that we would roll out of the house. Dinner at my mom's house was never about conversation and always about food. If there was casual banter among dinner guests, that was an added bonus.

My mom stood behind her chair and said, "So, what's so important?"

Great, her tone had gone from cheerful to annoyed. This was not a good way to start the conversation.

"I have some news for you. Well, actually, we have some news for you," I said. My eyes locked with my mother's.

She smiled and said, "Please don't make jokes. I know what you are going to say, and it's not funny. Now if you'll excuse me, the apple crumble needs to be removed from the oven, which is more important than your pregnancy joke."

My mom walked into the kitchen, leaving me, Sam, and my dad at the table. My dad shook his head and said, "I guess this is going to be harder than I thought."

I leaned my head back on my chair and stared up at the ceiling. I felt so full. I felt like my stomach was expanding as I sat there. I hoped the stomach expansion was not creating any stretch marks. My stretch mark thoughts were interrupted by Sam putting his hand on my shoulder and saying, "You never told me we were going to tell your parents today. If you want to tell them, that's fine, but let's call my parents and put them on speaker. We should tell everyone at the same time."

"We are not calling your parents right now. We are telling my mother as soon as she returns with dessert," I said firmly as I continued to stare up at the ceiling.

"But—" he started, when I cut him off and said, "No buts. We will tell your parents in person, and that's not up for discussion."

I could feel Sam's gaze on me. I knew he was raging inside, but my father was still seated beside us, so Sam didn't dare raise his voice. My dad broke the tense silence.

"I read that the cool air is here to stay for another week or so at least."

I couldn't care less about the weather, but I nodded politely and said in a quiet voice, "Yes, I heard that also."

My mom returned with the apple crumble, with Anna holding the ice cream and a teapot. Anna carefully poured the tea into dainty white cups with gold trim as my mother dished out the apple crumble.

We ate the apple crumble without saying much. The warm sweetness of the crumble combined with the cool ice cream made me feel completely at peace with the world in that moment. I could hear Anna in the kitchen scraping plates and loading the dishwasher.

My mom sipped her tea. "Aren't you going to drink your tea? I made sweetened chai just for you." My mom's sweet chai was rich with cream, spiced with cardamom, and sweetened with condensed milk. But I'd managed to cut out all coffee and was now trying to wean myself off tea. I rarely had tea or coffee at night anyway, since it would cause me to toss and turn throughout the night in bed. That would have made the perfect excuse for turning it down, but I needed to tell her the truth.

I simply said, "It's not a joke."

She glared at me, and her eyes started welling up in tears. She started clearing the dessert plates and forks from the table and took them into the kitchen. We all watched her in silence.

"Ma, aren't you going to say anything?" I asked. As she walked back and forth from the dining room to the kitchen, clearing dessert from the table, the only words she spoke were instructions to Anna on where to store the leftovers.

Finally, once the entire table had been cleared, and there was nothing else for her to focus on, she stood behind her chair and said, "How can you do this to me? After everything we have done for you, how can you ruin your life like this? We sent you to the best private schools even when we couldn't afford it, and now you are going to throw all of that away."

I'd known my mother would be upset, but I'd had no idea she would be this upset. Most mothers would hug their daughters and cry tears of joy. Not my mom.

"Ma, stop being ridiculous. I'm not throwing my life away; I'm going to have a baby. I'm finishing law school, and I will start working as soon as I can."

My mom didn't look convinced. She changed the topic of conversation and started giving me advice. "You will have to start eating healthy, balanced meals on a daily basis. Don't drink too much milk, or the baby will be very hairy."

This was the advice she was giving me? Old wives' tales from India? Her tone was sad, and her eyes held back tears. I wanted to leave; the air in the house was suffocating. There was no point sitting in the dining room any longer. I'd known she wouldn't be happy, but I'd never predicted she would be almost resentful.

"We're going to leave," I announced as I stood up from the chair. Sam also stood up. He likely had been wanting to leave anyway—he'd barely said two words during dinner.

My dad stood up to walk us to the door. My mother didn't move. "Bye, Ma," I said as I walked away.

"Bye," she replied, staying in her chair.

I was angry at her for reacting the way she had. As we stood in the entrance and put our coats on, my dad said, "Don't worry about her. She just needs time to digest this information. I'll talk to her." I wasn't convinced that my dad could help this time.

11

Sam and I drove almost the entire thirty-minute drive from our downtown condo to Brampton in silence. He was likely still too groggy from waking up earlier than usual to head to his parents' house for lunch, and I was caught up in thoughts about what had transpired at my parents' house the night before. I'd promised Sam we would tell his parents today, but I was concerned about how they would react. I knew his mother was obsessed with me having a child, but she knew I was in school and still had ample time to give her grandchildren, so she hadn't pressured us, aside from a few normal Indian-mother-in-law-type hints, like holding other people's kids and saying loudly, "I can't wait to have my own grandchild!"

We pulled up, and as we approached the house, the front door flew open, and about twenty relatives huddled in the entranceway. What was going on? I thought we were just meeting his parents for lunch and spending the afternoon with them. That usually meant sitting in the family room sort of watching television and sort of discussing the family business, which was all they talked about all the time. Which guy had bought which hotel in which city for whatever price was basically the only gossip they engaged in for entertainment value, when they weren't talking about serious business to do with their own hotels.

We were just a few feet away when loud Indian music started playing. I looked at Sam and saw that he had a huge smile on his face.

"What is going on?" I asked him under my breath while still trying to hold a smile, given that twenty of his elderly relatives were staring at us.

"I'm so sorry, but I called my mom this morning and told her we had big news. She guessed what it was, and she was so excited that I guess she told some of our family."

"Some" of the family? There were twenty people huddled at the door. His aunt held a tray with all sorts of stuff on it, like when we got married.

When we reached them, Sam's mother, Nina, grabbed my arms and pulled me close. She gave me a tight hug and whispered in my ear, "Thank you for giving me this special gift!" She was holding back tears and smiling at me like I had helped her win the fifty-million-dollar lottery jackpot or something.

As she released me from her tight hold, the family members who were gathered behind her started cheering and hugging each other. Nina dabbed her finger into a little cup of liquid and then touched my forehead to create an orange dot, and whispered, "Don't worry, it's really watery, so it won't show when you wipe it off." She knew I did not like these traditions at all. She then pressed colored rice onto the yellow dot and then put a pink Smartie in my mouth and hugged me. Then she gently pushed me toward Sam's dad, who had a big smile on his face. He gave me an awkward hug, and I was then pushed down the line of the remaining eighteen relatives who all wanted to hug and kiss and congratulate me.

I finally made my way to the end of the line of relatives. The music was turned off and replaced with the television. All the men filtered into the family room to watch television, while all the women congregated in the kitchen to prepare the food. The formal dining table was set with the good china, and I could see that my mother-in-law had catered lunch from one of the most expensive Indian restaurants in the city. Delicious aromas filled the air, and I suddenly grew hungry.

I stood between the kitchen and the family room, not really sure where to go, when Sam came up to me with a big smile on his face. He gently touched my arm and stared into my eyes.

"Thank you for making my parents so happy. They completely adore you."

I was sure it was more the baby inside me that they adored, but regardless, for the first time I felt excited. This baby had already brought so much joy to people's lives, regardless of my mother's opinion.

I planned to have lunch with my mom the next time I was in town. Enough time had passed since I'd dropped the pregnancy bomb on her that I thought I better make an effort to mend things with her. Versace greeted me at the door when I walked into the house, which instantly made me happy to be home. I carried him to the kitchen, where I found my mom stirring a pot and talking on the phone.

She moved the phone away from her mouth and said, "Go sit at the table. Lunch will be ready in about five minutes." I walked over to the table, which she had set perfectly for lunch. My mom insisted that every meal we had at the house required a properly set table. A casual lunch required a formal setting of a fork, knife, salad fork, and soup spoon. There was a side plate and a large plate and a soup bowl. There was also a crystal glass for each of us and napkins. On the counter were the dessert plates, dessert forks, cups, and saucers, as well as fresh napkins. Once a year, when we were growing up, we would order pizza for dinner, and even that required a fork and knife.

LAW GIRL'S BUMP IN THE ROAD

I sat Versace on the chair beside me, and he laid his head in my lap. The one unhygienic and improper thing my mother allowed at the table was our family dog with his rhinestone collar. She claimed that he was not like other dogs because she bathed him almost daily, sprinkled him with scented power, and brushed him multiple times a day. He was allowed to be around the dinner table, but he was only allowed to eat food out of his dog bowl on the floor.

I could hear her speaking half in English and half in Gujarati on the phone, and at times she spoke a few words in Kutchi, a slightly different dialect. I understood every word of both languages but couldn't speak either. I realized she must have been talking to her sister or one of her cousins.

"Not to worry, I will definitely tell her everything," I heard my mom say.

When she came into the room, my mom spooned carrot-ginger soup into our bowls as she started talking. "Now that you are pregnant, as your mother, it's my duty to give you advice. I just got off the phone with Auntie Yasmin, and before that Auntie Azina, and they both made me promise that I would tell you everything you need to know. They actually wanted to fly here to tell you in person, but I told them it was unnecessary and that I could handle it."

I was growing concerned about what kind of "advice" my mom's sister and cousin would provide, and with good reason. "First of all, you need to eat cucumber so your baby will be fair. And eat beets, because that will give him rosy cheeks. Oh, and my father says to tell you to eat lots of fish. He says that eating fish makes brains, and brains make money, and with money you can buy more fish!"

Really, my grandfather was giving me pregnancy advice?

"He also said to tell Sam that a pregnant woman should never be deprived of what she craves, or her baby boy will have a bent penis."

I somehow managed to avoid snorting carrot-ginger soup out my nose.

"Thanks, Ma. Can you maybe not ask my grandfather for pregnancy advice?"

"And Auntie Azina says to remind you to never put your baby in front of a mirror, or he'll be conceited."

"Why do you assume it's going to be a boy? I'm having a girl. I can tell."

"Please. Oh, and we can't forget the tea. After the baby is born, we need to make sure you drink the tea that will make your vagina tight again."

"Ma! Enough," I said. "Does this mean you're not upset anymore?"

"A child is a blessing, even if it doesn't always come at the best time. Besides, you're old enough, you're married..."

My mother recited the mantra I'd been telling myself. I guess we were both trying to sell ourselves on the idea. At least we had that in common.

12

Sam accompanied me to my second visit to the ob-gyn. He was excited about being with me and surprisingly nervous about the prospect of discovering our baby's sex. Until the last few weeks, Sam had been a strong believer in the old-school attitude that you should wait until the baby is born. But how could I decorate? How could I buy clothes? Of course, I already knew that the baby was a girl, but I needed proof.

I had read all the articles I could on how to determine the sex of your baby, many of them about old wives' tales. I had basically passed all the tests for a girl, including the fool-proof Chinese string trick. Then there was the fact that my hips and butt were growing faster than my stomach, which according to my mother's friends, indicated that it was a girl. I hadn't managed to satisfy the heart-rate test because I hadn't asked for the heart rate during my first ultrasound. Supposedly a fast heart rate would indicate a girl, while a slower one would indicate a boy. But everything, including my dreams, suggested that a beautiful baby girl was going to enter my life in a few months.

Actually, during the early weeks of my pregnancy, I'd had a vivid dream that I was at a Toronto Raptors game with my son. He was about six years old and wearing a Raptors jersey in purple, my favorite color. It was the dream I remembered most, but it didn't matter because I knew I was having a girl and was thrilled by the thought. There were so many beautiful girls' clothes to buy, and I couldn't wait to start shopping. I would teach my daughter the proper way to apply makeup, I would take her to the spa, and I'd let her borrow my clothes. I couldn't wait to have her sitting beside me while we both got mani-pedis. And Sam would look even more adorable with a little girl crawling all over him. I could picture our new happy family perfectly.

But both Mom's and Sam's families were Indian, so I had that to contend with. In Indian culture, the belief is that you should have a boy first because a boy continues the family lineage, and the parents eventually move in with him and his wife and grow old in their home. Girls, on the other hand, abandon their parents to enter another household when they marry. This was clearly ridiculous in the Western world, especially since often the opposite was true. I was even closer to my parents after marriage than I had been before, while my brother had always been closer to his girlfriend's than to our parents. I had already planned that my parents would live with me when they got older. I mean, what mother would want to live with her daughter-in-law—and vice versa? And even though a girl might not carry on her family's last name, it doesn't really make a difference. When you accomplished something, everyone knew who your parents were because they'd proudly make it known. The traditional Indian mentality didn't work for me at all.

My mom had been the first of her family of four siblings to have a child, and my grandmother had thought it was a terrible tragedy when I was born a girl. I believed that her unhappiness resulted in the real tragedy, a curse of sorts: her other eight grandchildren were all boys. My parents believed that having daughters is *lakshmi*, meaning that it brings wealth and prosperity. I agreed, so I was desperately hoping for a girl. I couldn't wait to find out for sure.

Sam was just as eager to find out the sex, but for a slightly different reason. I'd been referring to our unborn baby as "she," and it was driving him crazy. He said that if it was a boy, then I was confusing him with all this girl talk. After the ultrasound, if my suspicions were correct, I would be permitted to resume calling her "she."

I'd allowed Sam to come to the ultrasound appointment with me on the condition that he not embarrass me by asking thousands of ridiculous questions. The last time he'd said to the doctor, "Selena likes eating chocolate. Is eating chocolate permitted during pregnancy?" I'd almost died, partially out of fear that the doctor would say no.

We checked in with the lady at the front desk of the ultrasound clinic, who barely stopped chatting to the lady sitting beside her. Sam's cell phone rang, and he answered it. The two dozen people crowded in the small waiting room all turned and glared, likely due to the "no cell phone" signs posted everywhere. He kept repeating himself on the phone, getting louder and slower, like the person he was talking to wasn't hearing him or maybe he was cutting out, probably because we were in the lower level of the lower level of the hospital. I nudged him and gestured for him to leave the waiting area, since nobody wanted to listen to his conversation about a housekeeper who hadn't shown up for work at the hotel that day.

He wandered off, not pausing in his conversation, and seconds later my name was called. I looked around but couldn't find him. Great, now what was I supposed to do? The lady again called my name, and I walked over to her.

"Sorry, I was just looking for my husband. He had to take a call."

The lady was polite but firm. "We have people booked for appointments all day, and unfortunately we cannot wait. Either you have your ultrasound now or rebook for a few weeks from now."

I was not waiting a few weeks for the most exciting part of the pregnancy. "It's fine. I'll do it now."

I followed her to the ultrasound room. After she left, I took the thin blue gown off the hospital bed and stared at it. I wasn't sure which way was the front. I'd never actually been a patient before and had never had to wear one of these faded hospital gowns. How could sick people recover in such an unfortunate environment?

As I sat waiting for the lady to return, I started to wonder whether Sam would be able to find me. I pulled my phone out of my purse, but there was no service in the bunkerlike ultrasound room.

The door opened, and I dropped my phone back in my purse.

"All ready?" the technician asked with mild excitement.

"Yes, I'm ready."

"Time to lie down." I lay down on the bed with my head close to the monitor. "Come closer to me; don't be shy."

I wasn't being shy, but if I moved closer to her, then I wouldn't be able to see the monitor. Still, I complied. Then she pushed my gown off my belly. Now I was shy. I couldn't believe I was lying here, in this depressing, dimly lit room, exposing myself to a stranger. At least I'd kept my bra on.

She put a device on my belly. Maybe this was how she was going to tell if it was a boy or girl. She pressed a button, and then I heard it. It was not the gender-finding machine. The device she had put on my belly was a heart monitor. I was actually listening to my baby's heartbeat.

My eyes welled up with tears. This was my baby! There was a little thing living inside me! I felt so emotional, but for the first time, I had a knot in my throat and tears in my eyes because I was so excited, so happy, so badly wanting to hold this little baby in my arms. These were tears of joy and total bliss.

I had never cared much about other people's kids. I was not one to ooh and ahh over babies and gush about how adorable they were, but here I was with my own baby, and I was extremely excited.

"Baby's heart rate is normal." She squeezed clear jelly all over the wand, and it looked like lube. I suddenly felt more uncomfortable. Not only was I half naked in front of a stranger in a dimly lit room, but now she was squeezing lubricant on some foreign device to put who knows where. I stared up at the ceiling, trying not to look concerned or at least not let her see my discomfort. Then I felt a cold, squishy sensation on my belly. I looked down and saw the wand being moved over my tummy. Thank goodness; the lube wasn't for parts I normally associate lube with.

With the other hand, she tapped away on the keyboard, her eyes glued to the screen. I looked up at the screen and realized that this was the moment. She was verifying the sex. I could see the outline of my baby! This was incredible. I couldn't believe that this baby was actually in my tummy. Yes, my tummy was looser, and I felt fatter, but I hadn't formed a solid baby bump yet.

"You want to know the sex?" she asked.

"Yes, absolutely! Who wouldn't want to know?"

"Some people want a surprise."

I was not one of those people. I wanted to know.

"It's a boy!" she announced, with more enthusiasm than I had heard from her during our entire time together.

My gaze turned from looking at the lubed device on my belly to the screen and then to the lady. I was speechless. This could not be happening.

Right then the door to the room flung open, and my eyes shot to the door. I had forgotten about the awkward situation I was in and the gloomy room. It had been replaced by disappointment and now curiosity about who could possibly be at the door.

In walked Sam, and in a cheery voice he said, "What did I miss?"

I looked at him, and our eyes locked for a few seconds. I knew he could tell something had happened and that I wasn't happy. He immediately walked over to me and said quietly, as he took my hand in his, "What happened?"

Before I could say anything, the ultrasound technician said in a confident voice, "Would you like to see your baby? He appears to be healthy based on measurements, and he has a normal heart rate. Mom is also doing well, with normal blood pressure."

A smile grew in Sam's voice as he said, "Did you say 'he'? It's a boy?"

The lady replied, "Yes, it's most definitely a boy."

"Wow! That's amazing. It's a boy!" Sam said with delight. He became giddy and kept repeating "It's a boy." I was sure it was all he could do to stop himself from jumping up and down and screaming to the world that he was going to have a son.

The technician asked if we wanted to purchase ultrasound pictures, and she pulled out a price chart. "I can print this out on paper for free, but for proper pictures you will need to pay—"

I cut her off. "We'll take the free print." I just wanted to leave. I wanted to rip the stupid faded-blue hospital gown off and get the hell out of that dim, depressing room. I wanted to be outside. I needed fresh air to breathe.

She looked at me. "Is everything okay? The baby is perfectly normal. You have nothing to worry about." Her tone suggested genuine concern.

"I'm not concerned about the baby, I'm just feeling a bout of morning sickness and need some air," I lied.

"Oh, completely understandable. I'll leave the room so you can change." She passed me some sandpaper-like paper towel that she'd pulled off a roll so I could wipe the lubricant off my belly and then left the room.

Sam looked at me. "You are being ridiculous." He knew it wasn't morning sickness that was bothering me.

I couldn't look at him. I knew I wasn't reacting the way I should. I had a healthy baby boy growing inside me. I immediately felt guilty. I knew some people tried for years to get pregnant, and here I was annoyed by the gender of my first child. It just wasn't what I had planned.

Actually, nothing was the way that I had planned it: no pink and purple, no frills, no princess dresses, no mani-pedi dates, and let's not forget no job, no future career plans. Making matters worse, I knew my in-laws were going to be more possessive of me somehow. It was their first grandchild, and it was a boy. By Indian custom, this was huge. This would give them bragging rights among all their friends and family. Money could not buy the value placed on the first child or grandchild being a boy.

"Let's just get out of here." I wiped my stomach off as best I could with the hopelessly nonabsorbent paper towel and put my clothes on. As we walked out of the room, Sam turned to look back at me and said, "The first person we need to call is my mom. She is going to be beyond ecstatic." He hadn't stopped smiling since he'd learned the news. I walked slowly behind him with dizzying thoughts about the future swirling in my head.

13

After I finished my last law school exam, I walked to my apartment in a daze. Normally after writing an exam, my mind was racing with thoughts of the questions posed and the answers that I'd provided. I would pick up a textbook or call a friend to compare answers. Law-school exams were a bitch and a half, far worse than other exams I had written in the past. The key to answering questions was to use the FIRAC method—facts, issue, rule, analysis, and conclusion—and to write two-to-four-page answers. Even though I could have answered most questions in one page, if I'd done that, I would have failed. I found this frustrating because law school professors were usually academics, often somewhat removed from practice. I wondered whether lawyers actually used

FIRAC. I had no idea how what I'd learned at law school would be useful in real life.

As I walked home this time, I thought not about the exam but about the fact that I was done. I was actually done! I'd finished a program that most people had thought I wouldn't even start. I was so close to becoming a lawyer I could feel it. I could finally move back home. After seven years of university, I was finally finished studying on a full-time basis. There would be no more dinky apartments, late-night food runs, all-nighters, binge drinking (okay, maybe this would still happen), struggling to stay awake in class, volunteering for school clubs, or hanging out with friends in the halls. I had just completed seven amazing years of my life, and on the one hand I was so happy that it was over and that I could finally live with my husband and be close to my family. But on the other, I felt an overwhelming sadness. As my thoughts swirled, I felt tears streaming down my face. I started walking a little faster. I didn't want to see anyone or talk to anyone. I wanted to be alone and to cry alone, not in a depressed, pathetic way, but in a cleansing, feel-good way. I picked up the pace, jogging until I reached my apartment, and then I curled up on the sofa with a blanket, drifting off to sleep with my damp cheek stuck to my velvet cushion.

The ringing of my phone awakened me. I opened my eyes and had no idea what time it was. It was getting dark outside, so it was definitely evening.

I was hungry and confused and wasn't quite sure what to do. I thought about heading to Toronto right away, rather than waiting until the next day. All I had were a suitcase of clothes, some books, and a blanket and a few pillows. The sofa I was lying on belonged to my landlord. I hadn't used it all year because I'd thought it was dirty from being used by all the previous tenants, but the last couple of weeks it had served as my bed, my desk, and my dining room table as well as my sofa. I didn't have much, but I would have to make a few tiring trips to load my car with the leftover stuff.

I grabbed my bag and reached for my cell phone. It was seven; I had been asleep for three hours and missed two calls. Both were from my mom. She always called me after an exam to see how it went. She would also call me before, if my exam was in the morning, to make sure that I was awake. She'd started doing that during undergrad at my request. Thanks to Red Bull–fueled all-nighters, I would usually try to sleep for a couple of hours before the exam, so in addition to setting my phone alarm, I would ask my mom to call me. I'd had a roommate in undergrad who'd slept through an exam, and I never wanted that to happen to me. She'd luckily managed to schedule the exam on another date after crying, begging, and pleading with the professor, who had taken pity on her, but I didn't want to ever have to endure that.

I decided to head to Toronto that night. There was no reason to wait, and what would I do in Kingston? I had no television and nothing to do in my apartment. The only friends who were still in town were studying for exams.

I stood up from the sofa, stretched my arms, and smiled.

"I actually did it!" I said quietly but out loud. "Holy shit, I actually did it." My world was complete, and I was content.

I arrived in Toronto just after midnight. The drive from Kingston was only two and a half hours, but it took a while to load my car, drop my key off with the landlord, and stop at every rest area to use the washroom. The peeing thing was so annoying. I wasn't drinking that much more fluid, so I didn't understand why being pregnant made you pee more frequently.

I pulled into my spot in our condo parking garage, right beside Sam's car. He was likely awake, eating pizza, drinking a can of Coke, and watching a movie—usually what he was doing around this time. It didn't bother me because I didn't see it that often, since we'd only been living together part-time.

Things would be different now that I was moving home. I wasn't sure what to expect. I wasn't sure if he would start eating and sleeping better or whether I would have to tolerate his habits and he mine. Time would tell.

As I entered the elevator, my stomach started gurgling, and I felt like I was going to be sick. This little baby was not easing up on my system.

I walked into the condo, and Sam jumped up from the sofa to greet me.

"Hi, sweetie!" he said enthusiastically.

"Hi," I said, trying to sound excited but failing miserably.

"What's wrong? Aren't you excited?"

"Of course," I replied. "I can't believe I finally finished law school!"

I saw his smile fade. "I meant, aren't you excited to finally move home and be with me as my wife?"

"Oh, of course I am," I said quickly. "I'm just really tired right now. I'm not thinking straight. You know, I had my last exam today, and then I had to load my car with everything still left in my apartment, then the drive back, and now the baby is making me feel queasy."

Sam's enthusiasm returned. "Well, how about you come sit with me. I just started this movie and I ordered a pizza and wings. Let me get you a slice."

The last thing I wanted was pizza. I was certain that I would in fact vomit if I went near it.

"I think I'm just going to head to bed," I said as politely as I could. Sam could finally see that I wasn't feeling great, so he hugged me and helped me with my bags. After a quick shower, I sank into our cozy bed with relief. I was home.

14

Not long after, I started both my sixth month of pregnancy and the Bar Admissions Course, which consisted of daily classes throughout the summer, plus eight exams. I had to do this before I had my baby if I stood any chance of becoming a lawyer any time soon. The course would be filled with hundreds of students from law schools scattered across the country. I needed to wear clothes that made me look professional and put together, at least for my self-esteem.

I stood in front of my closet, scanning all the clothes that were hanging there. Nothing fit, especially all the wonderful things I'd bought in New York City just a few months ago. Instead of making me look pregnant, they made me look pudgy.

Finding clothes to wear during the course was only one fashion crisis, however. My graduation from law school was looming. One week before the ceremony, I scoped countless stores at the mall, spending hours searching every women's clothing store. I refused to wear maternity clothes. I wanted to wear something sophisticated but not too boring, and I was convinced I could squeeze my expanding stomach into normal clothes.

I bought the outfit four days before the ceremony, since I'd been nervous that if I bought it any further in advance, it wouldn't fit. I ended up buying an off-white linen pant suit and a camel-colored linen sleeveless top with a floral print that matched the color of the suit perfectly. When I'd tried on the pants, I'd held them up in the air to examine the size of the waist. The pants looked massive. I'd never imagined I would purchase anything so big and kept telling myself, "You're pregnant, not large."

When I got home, I laid everything out on my bed to make sure that it was the perfect outfit for my perfect graduation day. I picked up the shoes I'd bought—off-white-and-camel heels—and a thought dawned on me. These were really high heels. I had been wearing heels my entire pregnancy, but I hadn't been walking in front of an audience. I usually didn't get nervous in front of crowds, but being pregnant at a university graduation ceremony, in front of a huge audience staring at me while I walked across a stage, was something that might make even me a little nervous. Oh God, what if the baby decided to start kicking and threw me off-balance, and I flew across the stage? Well, given that I'd be wearing a giant muumuu of a gown over my pregnant belly, I certainly wasn't going to wear flats. I would look so frumpy.

The day arrived. The ceremony was starting at eleven in Kingston, so Sam, my parents, and I piled into the car at eight in the morning, which would leave me with a little time to get my gown and get into line backstage. I had decided to wear sweatpants in the car so I wouldn't crease my linen suit. I'd also decided not to put my makeup on because pregnancy was making my skin oily rather than glowy, and I'd just have to reapply it after I got out of the car anyway. So time was tight.

We had been in the car for less than five minutes when Sam's phone started ringing. That damn thing was always ringing. The calls were mostly from family and friends, but the hotels would call him if they couldn't reach his parents. This call was from a front desk employee at their downtown Toronto hotel. Apparently, he was having difficulty with the computer and needed a password, so Sam said he would be there in a minute.

Nobody said anything, and Sam didn't dare look at me. I think everyone could feel my irritation. I had planned everything and worked with timetables, but Sam liked being spontaneous and was always throwing off my schedule. I liked to be a few minutes early, but he was always late by almost an hour. One would think that I would come to accept his tardiness as part of who he was, but that was not the case. I felt that it should work the other way: that with time he would understand the importance of being early, or at least on time. The result was numerous arguments on the subject.

We pulled up to the hotel, and Sam said, "I'll be back in a minute." A minute, my ass, I thought. Fifteen minutes later, my excited parents were getting a little nervous. My mom checked her watch, and my dad got out of the car and started pacing. Watching my parents was only making my anger turn into rage. This was the day that I had been waiting for, the end of a quarter of a century of nonstop formal education, and my husband was ruining it.

My mom interrupted my angry thoughts. "Well, I guess this is the best time to give you your graduation gift. I wanted to give it to you after the ceremony, but then you wouldn't be able to make use of it today, so here you are."

She put her hand in her purse and pulled out a little turquoise box. I knew the box well. Every girl knows that box. A smile quickly appeared on my face. Inside were classic roman-numeral-design Tiffany earrings and a matching bangle, exactly what I'd wanted. I removed my pearl studs and replaced them with my new earrings, then pulled out a compact from my purse so I could look at myself in the mirror.

"Thanks, Ma," I said, too happy to say more.

"Darling, you don't know how proud we are of you. We are so happy that today has finally arrived. We are finally able to say that all that money we spent on your education was worth it." My parents had been sending me to the best private schools in the city since I'd started at Montessori when I was eighteen months old. At times, my parents had encountered financial difficulties, but education for me and my brother was one thing that they refused to sacrifice. I only hoped that I could provide my children with the same education.

Finally, Sam appeared. He had taken twenty minutes, which meant that I was going to have only a few minutes to grab my gown, change, and get into line. I was dreading the thought of being frazzled on a day like this. If only the procession would start late, although that wasn't likely. Queen's was a university of tradition, which meant that everything had to be proper, and starting late would certainly not be proper.

We had been driving for about an hour when I suddenly felt the urge to pee, of course. I leaned forward and said to Sam, "We need to stop at the next exit. I have to use the washroom."

"The next rest stop is in about fifteen minutes. Can you wait until then? Because there is a Wendy's and Tim Hortons there, and I'm starving."

"I would *love* a coffee right now!" my mom chimed in enthusiastically.

"I could get some fries to tide me over," said my dad.

We took the exit off the highway and headed toward the law school. The issue, however, was that we had fifteen minutes to get there, which was exactly how long the drive should take. I still needed to change and apply my makeup and poof up my hair a bit, and I was sure it would also be a chore to find parking. I felt so annoyed that on perhaps the most important day of my life to date, a milestone moment, I was arriving late.

"We're in Kingston!" Sam announced cheerfully. He knew very well that we were running late for the ceremony but avoided mentioning that fact.

"Where am I supposed to change? I can barely move around in the car with this extra weight in my midsection. Regardless, I hope you didn't think I was actually going to change in the car." I had planned on changing in the restroom at the law school, but I didn't want to rush in late for my ceremony and let everyone see that I wasn't even ready for the procession.

"I know—we'll stop at my friend's hotel on Princess." Sam seemed to have "friends" everywhere.

"Okay," I said reluctantly.

We pulled up to what looked more like a seedy motel. Sam parked under the awning of the main entrance and jogged inside. Moments later he came out with a room key and got back in the driver's seat.

"We've got one-oh-two, just next to the front desk. I told him we would be five minutes and only using the washroom so he wouldn't need a housekeeper to go in after. Don't make a mess!"

Obviously, I wasn't going to make a mess. I didn't even have time to make a mess. Sam started the car and parked in front of the room, a driving distance of a whole twenty feet. I rolled out of the car, grabbed my clothes, and ran into the room, where in five minutes I managed to change clothes, apply some makeup, and fluff up my hair with wet hands. I ran back to the car, and we were off.

Sam stopped in front of the law school. "How about you all get out and I'll go park," he said. As I ran from the car, I heard my mom yell, "We love you!" and my heart melted a little. I suddenly realized that I was running in heels with a huge belly. I felt enormous and completely unsteady on my feet. I also felt out of breath because, on top of it all, of course, I was out of shape.

Inside I found the lineup of law students moving toward the interior room where the ceremony was being held. The sound of the door opening and the clicking of my heels made the whole procession turn to see who it was. They seemed to stare a lot longer than they needed to.

"Just me, giant pregnant Selena. Nothing to see here."

I couldn't blame them for staring, though. They hadn't seen me in a month, and I was a lot larger than when they'd last seen me. I was also the only person who was pregnant.

Of course, the first person to say anything to me was picture-perfect Jane.

"Selena, hurry up and get in line. You need to put your gown and cap on."

I grabbed the gown and cap and started putting them on as I ran to the front of the line to find my place in the alphabet. The line kept moving, but slowly, so I was able to find my spot.

"Selena, you made it," said Ethan in an excited voice as he held the line up to let me in behind him.

"Yeah, just barely, I guess."

"Don't worry, you haven't missed anything."

I immediately felt better. He was right; I hadn't missed anything. But I was panting, and as we walked into the room I noticed I was sweating. Why was this happening? The black gown was heavy, but we were in an air-conditioned building. I realized that it must have been the excess weight I was carrying, combined with the forced exercise. In fact, ever since I'd gotten pregnant, it had felt like my antiperspirant had stopped working. I wouldn't be able to lift my arm up much to accept my degree or the dean would get a whiff of undeodorized armpit.

We took our seats at the front of the theater, and as I looked up to watch the dean give the opening address, it hit me. This was my day! I'd made it, not only to the ceremony, but to this point in life. For the first time during my pregnancy I felt like I was truly glowing, regardless of the fact that there was a chance I would trip and fall on the stage due to my insistence on wearing heels or the fact that I might have smelled like I hadn't taken a shower in a few days. It didn't matter because I was almost a real-life lawyer. I was smiling both inside and out. Maybe my baby was smiling too.

15

It was time to seriously put my mind to essentials. Scouring the Internet, reading books and magazines, and attending baby shows had proven completely daunting and potentially very expensive. Did babies need bookshelves especially made for them, or was Ikea sufficient? Did I need a special diaper garbage can, or could I just buy any garbage can? Strollers, car seats, bottles, cribs...I was overwhelmed. I tried desperately to make a list and research the essentials, but I just couldn't focus. How was I going to work with a newborn, and how were we going to afford all this stuff? I knew that our parents would pay for everything if we asked, but I wanted us to do this ourselves, as new parents.

I started to make a list of the essentials that we required immediately: bottles, sterilizer, car seat, stroller, crib, diapers, wipes, onesies, soap. It was eleven in the morning. I had already eaten breakfast, cleaned the condo, and made a to-do list, and now I wanted to act on it. I went into the bedroom to wake Sam, as he was still asleep.

"Time to get up, honey. Lots to do today," I whispered as I shook his shoulder. There was no movement. What time had he gone to bed? I wondered. I tried again, this time shaking him more rigorously and pleading in a normal voice, "Please wake up."

Sam finally stirred, responding with, "I need another hour."

"Another hour?" Seriously? It was already late enough. "The stores aren't open that late today. It's Saturday, and we have so much to look at." Sam turned over, his back to me. I felt my inner rage building. I already felt overwhelmed by all we needed to do. I wasn't sure how we would pay for all this stuff, and now my husband was more interested in sleeping. If he slept another hour, then we wouldn't leave the condo for at least two hours, leaving us with only a couple of hours before shops closed.

I left the room and called my mom. I had a knot in my throat from holding back tears when she answered.

"Hi, sweets!"

That's all it took—tears started streaming down my face. I guess she heard my little crying breaths because, before I could say anything, she asked, "What's wrong? What happened?"

"Ma, I need to buy all this baby stuff, and Sam is still asleep, and I don't know where to start, and shops will be closed in a few hours, and tomorrow we have to go to a family luncheon at his parents' house."

My mom said very calmly, "Don't worry. We'll come over! What is most important from the list for today?"

I scrolled through the list. "I think we should get the crib because I also need help building it." My dad was an amazing handyman. I don't think guys are built that way these days, or at least none that I have come across.

"Okay, we'll be over in about twenty minutes." I felt instant relief as I got off the phone.

We went to a crib manufacturing outlet not far away, and I scored a high-end crib for half the retail price. Even my frugal father was impressed.

"Where did you find this place?"

"Online," I said proudly.

A tall man greeted us. He showed us the various cribs available and explained in his east-coast drawl that it was his company, started when his wife had been pregnant with their first child. They now had five young children under the age of ten.

"Is this crib going into that car?" he asked when he brought it outside.

"Yes," I replied shyly. We packed up my dad's S class Mercedes with the crib, which looked a little ridiculous. I was squished in the backseat with boxes of crib parts, and I instantly felt like a kid again—except I was carrying my own kid now. I couldn't stop the tears from running down my face.

My mom could barely see me with all the boxes surrounding me, but she noticed my tears. "What's wrong?" she asked.

"I just can't believe that he is missing all of this. Shouldn't I be buying a crib with my husband? I feel like a fifteen-year-old single mom." This was not how I'd envisioned that things would be. Actually, I had never really put much thought into what it would be like to prepare for a baby because I thought I was years away from it. But here I was on the brink of motherhood, still relying on my parents. I guess if my career as a lawyer didn't work out, I could try out for that teen mom show. Oh wait, that wasn't even an option, since I was twenty-five.

As I stared out the window, my mind swirling in many different directions, I casually said out loud, "Maybe I should stay home for a bit, in my own bed, in my own bedroom"

Before I could even expand on that thought, my mother interjected. "We weren't sure when to tell you, but maybe now is a good time."

My gaze turned from the window to my mom. "Tell me what?" I asked with slight concern. I had thought my parents would be excited by the idea of me staying at home for a while. They always complained that their big house felt so empty without my brother and me around.

"Your father and I have decided to sell the house."

"Seriously? You are actually going to move? But all my stuff is there, and you love that house! How can you just up and move?" The idea that my parents would one day sell our family home had never entered my mind. That house was our foundation. It was where I went when I wanted comforting, it was my safe place, and I knew my parents felt the same way. My brother had never seemed as attached, but I'd always just assumed that was because he was a guy and didn't display his affection for things the same way as I did.

I had so many questions to ask my parents. "Have you even thought about where you'll move if you sell the house? You always said you couldn't imagine staying in a small home with neighbors after being spoiled with the property."

Again, my mom cut me off. "Your father and I have decided that we are moving to Vancouver."

"Excuse me? My father and you? Do you mean you? Why are you moving back to Vancouver? What's the deal with your obsession with BC? You move there every few years and then realize that the gloomy weather depresses you and that you miss Toronto and move back."

There was no way my father had anything to do with this decision, and I couldn't understand why he was keeping quiet. How could they leave me like this and sell the house at the same time? I was so upset, I just wanted to escape from the car and get this dumb crib up to the condo. I could take it up myself. How heavy could it be? Besides, Sam would build it one of these days...well, maybe he would, or he would hire someone or something. I felt so alone. I just wanted to be in Sam's arms.

My mom chimed in. "You are all grown up. You are going to be fine, and Sam's parents would really appreciate it if you were closer to them. That's not going to happen if we stay in town."

Was my mother trying to convince me that she was moving away for my benefit? This was completely ridiculous. Sometimes I just didn't understand how my mother was my mother.

16

I had planned to take prenatal classes with Sam during August because I'd figured that the Bar Admissions Course would be winding down then, as would Sam's work schedule. During my first trimester, when I had told Sam that I thought it would be fun to take these classes, he'd sort of laughed and said, "Well, I think you can have fun on your own." I remembered feeling devastated by his reaction. I mean, this was his child too. Didn't he want to participate in the process? As my pregnancy continued, he'd realized how much he wanted to know, and he'd agreed that completing the classes in August was a good idea so that we wouldn't forget anything by September when the baby was born.

We were both somewhat uncomfortable with the idea of prenatal classes. Although we generally got along well with others, I wasn't so sure how I would fare with other pregnant women. Most of the women I had met at the doctor's office and at prenatal yoga were significantly older than me, and I felt as if they looked at me with a disapproving eye. They all seemed to know each other from mommy groups or neighborhoods. Again, I felt like I had been knocked up. Was I becoming insecure, or was this really how women were looking at me?

The second week in July seemed like a good time to call to schedule the classes, so I sat at my desk at home and looked through the "pregnant" file in my filing cabinet for the pamphlet containing information about birth preparation classes. Birth Preparation for Couples—$215. Wow, that was kind of more than I had anticipated. That was double the price of the Pumas I had bought a couple of months ago that Sam had blasted me for, saying that I didn't need more shoes. I wondered if he would have the same reaction to the price of the classes because I wouldn't even have a tangible item to show for the cost. But there was no question I had to enroll.

I called the phone number, and a friendly voice answered.

"I'm interested in enrolling in birth preparation classes."

"What month would you like to start the classes?"

"Next month, in August."

"Oh, I'm sorry, but we're completely full during August. We are booking in the new year."

"By new year, you mean in January?"

"Yes, that would be the new year, dear."

"But I kind of have to do them in August," I pleaded. "I'm due in September."

"That could be a problem," the woman responded.

"I thought I was calling well in advance. I didn't realize that there would be a waiting list."

"Well, dear, just to give you an idea, earlier today a woman called to schedule classes, and she's not due until February."

You mean I was supposed to call in my first trimester? "Is there anything you can do? My husband and I don't know anything."

There was a pause and then a deep sigh. "I can squeeze you in next weekend."

A whole weekend trapped in a hospital conference room with strange couples. Great. This woman thought that she was doing me a favor, and I guess she was, but I was double-minded about the whole thing.

The woman on the phone asked for my name.

"Selena Dean, I mean Khan. I mean Selena Khan." I must have sounded ridiculous to not even know my own name, so I tried to explain myself. "My husband and I don't see eye-to-eye on the name issue. You see, I haven't really changed my name, so I use my maiden name for work-related stuff, and I use his name when it's for family and his work stuff. He gets agitated on the issue, so I want to use his name since he'll be attending the classes."

"I see," the woman said. "I hope he's not acting in this manner on other issues, particularly during your pregnancy."

Oh, God. I immediately realized from the woman's tone that she thought Sam was abusive or something. Although I was a little amused by the allegation, I didn't want her thinking this.

"Dear," she continued, "if you ever need support from an outsider, please do not hesitate to call me, and I can put you in touch with a person who can help."

Not this again. "Thanks," I mumbled, rolling my eyes and getting off the phone as quickly as I could.

We were supposed to be in the hospital meeting room at nine o'clock in the morning. Helen, the teacher, had stated that explicitly. But getting Sam out of bed was not an easy task. There were ten couples registered for the class, including us, which meant that when we walked in at nine fifteen, eighteen people turned to look at us.

The nineteenth person, a lady in her late fifties wearing a large, floral hippie-type dress, came to greet us.

"Hi, there! I'm Helen. Welcome to prenatal class! Please print your name on a sticker over there and join the group."

I looked back to the group that was staring at us as we stood in the entrance of the meeting room. These people didn't look anything like us. They were all older, for one. All the women looked like they were in their thirties or forties, heavily pregnant and casually dressed.

Helen returned to the group and said, "Okay, where were we? Ah yes, listing our fears. Well, let's keep going. Shout them out as they come to you."

Sam came up to me and handed me a sticker. He had printed our names on the labels in his chicken scratch, which I didn't love, but it was nice of him to take care of it. As we sat down in the two empty chairs in the circle, I looked up at the flip chart containing the list that Helen had been making. Fears: childbirth, being a good parent, installing a car seat, changing diapers, breastfeeding.

Helen looked over to us. "Would you like to share your fears? It will enable me to focus on these areas a little more over the next two days."

I most definitely had fears—stretch marks, not getting my body back fast enough, not getting a job as soon as possible, et cetera. I opened my mouth to say something, and then closed it. Perhaps I should keep my fears to myself.

"The list pretty much sums up my main fears."

That was a complete lie. I had no concerns about being a good parent. I knew I would be an amazing parent.

Changing diapers? Seriously, that was someone's fear? Installing a car seat? I read that the best thing to do was to pay twenty dollars to get a professional to install your car seat. I already had a list of baby stores that provided this service. Childbirth would probably have scared me if I had been thinking about it, but my mind had been consumed with "my" fears up to that point.

"What about you, Sam? Care to share your concerns with the group?"

Everyone turned to look at Sam.

"Actually, yes, I have a few things I would like to add."

I turned to look at Sam too, my eyes wide. My concern immediately became what was about to come out of his mouth.

"I have no idea how to hold a baby. Like, what if I drop it? I don't want to drop it, but what if I'm holding the baby, and I reach for something and then need my other hand and forget that I'm holding this baby? I could just drop it!"

There were a few chuckles from the guys in the group. One guy named Jack chimed in and said, "Yeah, I could actually see that happening if I was watching football while sitting on my sofa and then reached for the remote control and then needed my other hand to grab a beer. I could see the baby just rolling out of my arms as I lean forward to get these essential items from the coffee table." Jack tried to demonstrate the scenario, and the entire class laughed. I could not tell if Jack was being sarcastic or serious.

In any event, Helen did not like how she'd lost control of the class. The guys were all suggesting dumb scenarios in which they could see themselves dropping a baby. Making matters worse was that they were all demonstrating these ridiculous scenarios. The women were silent as the men bonded.

"I think we need to refocus here," Helen said firmly. "Sam, thank you for sharing. I will add 'correctly holding a baby' to the list of fears." The fun was over, and Helen was back on track.

I looked at Sam again and saw a smile on his face. I knew that mischievous smile. He was proud of himself because he'd succeeded in lightening the mood and making the class have fun for a few minutes. He didn't have a fear of dropping the baby; he was just playing around. We could be anywhere, anytime, and he would enjoy life and make friends with ease. I loved that about him.

Three hours passed, I was bored and so hungry. We had covered all the fears on the list and more. For the last hour, the women would be lying on the mat and practicing different stretches, positions, and breathing techniques for labor while our partners were supposed to assist. Everyone helped move the chairs out of the way and mats were put down on the floor.

Sam helped me down on the mat, and then his phone rang.

"It's one of the hotels. I need to take this."

"Okay," I said as he left the room.

Helen began. "Use a pillow to prop yourself up. Let's start with deep inhales and loud exhales." I felt like I was in a yoga class. "Now, partners, start by placing your hands on the shoulders and gently massaging."

Sam was not back. Helen was walking around to each couple to correct breathing and suggest massage techniques, but just before she got to me, Sam returned.

"I gotta go. There's money missing from the downtown hotel. Text me when you're done here. I probably won't be back before this class ends."

He started making another call and left the room. Had he just left me here by myself during the partner activity? I was so angry.

As I looked around at all the pitying faces looking my way, I realized that apparently the whole class was aware of what had just happened. I was mortified. I wanted to leave, but I couldn't even get up from the mat without someone helping me and my giant belly up. I was a beached whale.

Then I felt comforting hands on my shoulders. "Dear, inhale...and exhale. It's going to be okay," Helen whispered. I wasn't sure if she was talking about childbirth or Sam abandoning me in class, but it was likely the latter.

It was finally one o'clock. Sam was nowhere to be seen. Some of the couples chatted with each other and some were chatting with Helen, talking about due dates, names, and other baby banter. I did not want to talk to anyone, so I snuck out as fast as possible and took the subway home. I wanted to eat and sleep and forget about the humiliation of Sam leaving me alone at the moment when I needed him most, not bothering to even come back. I was not going back for the second day of prenatal class. I would deal with Sam later.

Before she got on the plane for Vancouver to house hunt, my mom turned to me and said, "Selena, I almost forgot to tell you. I was reminded of something you absolutely must do during the last couple of months of your pregnancy." My mom seemed very serious, and I was growing concerned. "You must drink a cup of warm milk mixed with a tablespoon of melted butter every evening before bed."

I thought that perhaps she was joking. What could this possibly do for me, besides pack on the pounds and make it that much harder to get my prepregnancy body back?

"My aunt was a midwife years ago, and she reminded me to give you this advice."

"Why, Ma? What is the purpose?"

"Drinking this daily for at least the last two months will help you during labor. The baby will slide out more easily."

"You can't be serious. You can't possibly believe all this Indian hocus-pocus. Ma, the digestive tract and the vaginal canal aren't connected—not sure if you missed that in school!"

"Selena, don't be so stubborn. I did it with both you and your brother and had little difficulty getting you both out."

How was this the important message my mother was leaving me with? My parents both hugged me as best they could over my big belly and then joined the line to go through security at the airport. My mom looked back and blew a kiss to me.

17

Weeks passed of going through the motions of life as an unprepared pregnant girl. Sam continued to work, sleep, eat, and socialize. I continued to study for the bar exam and read a baby book that my mom had bought for me before she had left. Admittedly the book was a good read. I finally had a voice sharing her experiences with me week by week, someone I could relate to. I didn't have any friends with kids and I hadn't joined online mommy groups. All the women in the groups I'd come across were so excited about their upcoming babies. Surely I couldn't share my feelings with them. I was worrying about passing the bar and becoming a lawyer; for now, the baby seemed like the least of my worries given all the hard work I'd put in over the last seven years was on the line. Was I even retaining information when I studied? How long did I have to stay home with this baby before I could start working? How long would it take to lose the weight so I could look good for interviews? I was smart enough to know that these were questions I couldn't ask in mommy groups.

As I sat on the sofa eating a bowl of oatmeal, my one and only breakfast option given that I was suffering from severe constipation for the first time in my entire life—the pain of which is only truly imaginable if you've never experienced it—Sam's phone rang. He was still asleep, so I glanced at it and saw his sister's name on the screen. I wondered why she was calling, given that it was nine on a Sunday morning and she knew her brother well enough to know he'd still be asleep.

I thought about ignoring the call because I wasn't sure what mood she was going to be in. Nadya was always so moody. Most days she was angry at the world for no reason, and then at times she was happy as if she had never been angry. She was an extremely attractive girl, with golden brown, soft, curly hair and greenish-blue eyes the color of tropical water. Yet for some reason she was insecure and always angry. When I'd married her brother, she'd been angry at me because she felt that I had taken her brother away from her. The sad part is that I was excited to finally have a sister. Unfortunately, my sister-in-law had soon made it clear that she was not going to be my "sister." I kept my distance and secretly hoped that one day she would be my best friend like the sister I'd never had.

With my bowl of oatmeal in one hand, I picked up the phone on the last ring before it went to voice mail.

"Hi, Nadya!"

There was a pause, probably because she'd been hoping to hear Sam's voice. "Hi, Selena," she said with fake enthusiasm. "Is my brother there?"

"Yes, but he's asleep."

"Oh, I was hoping he would be awake. I was just making plans for the day and was wondering if he wanted to go buy the stroller."

Was she implying that she was going to buy *my* stroller with *my* husband and without me? Was there some other pregnant family member that she and my husband needed to buy a stroller for?

"Are you talking about buying a stroller for my baby?" I asked calmly despite the rage that was building inside.

"Yes, I'm buying a stroller for my nephew."

Given that she was still in university, what she really meant was that her parents were buying a stroller for my baby, and it seemed like I was getting squeezed out of the decision-making process on the purchase. Was this really happening?

Before I could say anything, Nadya added, "Also, my mom asked me to give you a list of names for her first grandson."

A list of names? She was buying my stroller *and* choosing my son's name?

"Why does your mom have a list of names?" I asked, dumbfounded.

"Didn't Sam tell you? Maybe you don't know, but it's tradition that the paternal grandparents choose the name of their first grandchild, especially if it's a boy." I didn't even know if this was true; regardless, it wasn't happening.

I couldn't believe this was happening. I didn't mind getting input on names, but I had to let them choose a name for my son? It would for sure be a traditional Indian name and most likely one that I didn't like. I started to wish that I had never answered the call.

"How about I get Sam to call you when he wakes up?" I wanted to end the conversation before she started to make other unwanted life decisions for me.

"Actually, I'm about fifteen minutes away, so not to worry, I'll get him out of bed. I know how you hate trying to get him up."

Of course I hated trying to get him up, because we had stuff to do like normal people, but he always preferred to sleep.

"You're coming over now? We were going to take care of some baby things today," I said as politely as I could, hoping she would get the hint that I didn't want her to come over.

"We *are* taking care of some baby things—we're getting the stroller today," she replied.

I could tell that I wasn't going to win this argument. She was coming up to my condo, she was going to wake my husband up, and we were going to have to bring her with us today.

After I hung up, I tried to force myself to eat more oatmeal in a desperate attempt to help with the bathroom situation. My stomach was so full and uncomfortable. Just inhaling air as I breathed made it feel like my belly was stretching. Oh geez, was I getting stretch marks as I breathed? For a second, I was able to escape my anger and instead focus on my constipation and possible stretch-mark situation. I wasn't sure which situation was worse.

It was two o'clock by the time we left the condo and almost three o'clock when we arrived at the specialty baby store. We had two hours before the store closed, but when we walked in, we discovered the place was full of people trying out rocking chairs, looking at cribs and high chairs, and paying careful attention to sales staff talking about different bottle lines, breast pumps, and sterilizers. I instantly felt overwhelmed and wanted desperately to walk out of the store. I didn't want to learn about all this stuff; I had the bar exam to study for. I didn't have the money for all these things, and all the couples who were shopping looked much older and so excited. I didn't belong there.

Nadya was already walking in with Sam as I froze in the entranceway. She turned back and said, "Aren't you coming in?"

I followed them to the stroller section, an area of the store that looked like a parking lot. There were two rows of fifteen strollers each, perfectly lined up as if they were shiny new cars in a showroom. The feature sheets outlined everything, and the prices ranged from a Toyota to a Mercedes. There was even one stroller off to the side, on a stage, that I assumed was the Rolls-Royce. Sam and Nadya started pulling strollers out from their parking spots and pushing them around to test the feel and the smoothness as I watched. I already knew I wanted a Bugaboo, but I also already knew that it was the Mercedes. I didn't want to test all those other strollers.

Now Nadya was pulling out a three-wheel one that looked like a stroller for sporty moms. I definitely did not need that SUV-type stroller. I did my running on the treadmill while watching *Housewives* of somewhere or other.

Nadya interrupted my thoughts. "You know I'm buying the stroller for my nephew, right?"

"Yes, you mentioned that," I replied. "It's really very nice of you, and we appreciate it." The truth was that I did appreciate that Sam's family was taking care of the purchase, but what I couldn't handle was that this entailed their input in the selection of the stroller. And then it happened.

"So basically," Nadya added, "I think this is the one."

I looked at the clunky contraption that was bright orange and thought, surely she must be kidding. Did I look like I wanted to push a pumpkin-colored stroller around the downtown streets? It would stick out among all the trendy black ones and not in a good way. Besides, all the dirt would show on that bright color.

"I'm not sure about the brand," I replied.

"Oh," she said as she rolled her eyes and turned toward Sam.

He looked at me and said, "Selena, we can look at other brands, but only if they have that color and are the same price and style. We don't need to get some high-end stroller when you are just paying for the name. A good-quality stroller that gets you from Point A to Point B is exactly what we need."

Nadya added, "I have just spent the last ten or eleven minutes test driving all of them, and this is the one."

Was she serious? I had spent hours researching every detail online—aesthetics, safety rating, recalls, brands, web forum opinions—and now she was telling me that "test driving" for ten or eleven minutes was going to be the basis for the stroller purchase?

As I kept my thoughts to myself, Nadya walked over to a store clerk who was finally available. The lady walked over and introduced herself to Nadya and Sam.

"You must be the proud parents!" she said enthusiastically.

"Um, I'm the mom," I said, raising my hand without thinking. I jerked it back down—it's not like I had to ask permission, after all.

"Oh, right. I understand you are looking at this model over here."

"*They* were," I replied, "but I was thinking more along the lines of a black Bugaboo like the one down the aisle."

Nadya and Sam looked at me and then looked at each other. Nadya pursed her lips and said, "Black is morbid, and the baby will overheat in the summer." Since most strollers were dark in color, I thought her comments were ridiculous and knew immediately that we had just entered power-struggle territory. Why she wanted me to get a pumpkin-spice-latte-colored stroller was beyond me, and it just wasn't my style. Purchasing a stroller is a lot like buying a car. They basically wanted me to sport an orange Honda, which wasn't happening. I wanted my baby in a black Lamborghini, and I wasn't agreeable to compromising on an orange one, even if it existed. Who buys an orange Lamborghini anyway?

The lady walked over to the Bugaboo floor model and pulled it out for me. She started to walk us through all the accessories that were available for purchase along with the prices. It was like we were being offered tints, additional speakers, upgraded rims, heated seats, rearview camera, and on and on, and it all seemed so unnecessary.

As the lady continued, I noticed I had tuned out until suddenly Nadya said, "Thank you for showing us this model, but we've made a decision. We are going to take the other one, and it's going to be in orange." Nadya had admittedly chosen a good stroller and still high-end, but not the one I wanted. Who was she to decide what stroller my son would be rolled around in? She reached into her purse and pulled out her wallet, then handed a credit card over and asked the lady if the stroller was in stock or if we had to pick it up another day.

Was this seriously happening? Was anyone going to ask me what *I* wanted? Sam and Nadya followed the lady to the cash register as I stood there, furious.

"Sam," I whispered under my breath. He didn't hear me. I lunged forward and grabbed his arm. Nadya noticed and turned around with the evilest glare plastered on her face, as if to say, "How dare you grab my brother's arm!"

"Why are we getting this stroller? I want the Bugaboo. Why aren't you asking me what I want? It's my baby that's in this large tummy."

"My sister is buying us this stroller, so it's her choice, and she has chosen a good-quality, colorful stroller, so don't you think you should be grateful?"

No, I didn't think I needed to be grateful! Why was he siding with her? Why didn't he care about my feelings? I felt rage coming over me, the type that starts in your gut and rises. The type that makes your whole body burn with fury. Enough was enough.

"Take me home now!" I said loudly enough that nearby couples turned around, cheery faces turning into shocked stares. I was too angry to care.

Sam was immediately furious. "It's not just your baby! This is my family's first grandchild, and it's a boy, which makes it even more special. This is my family's baby whether you choose to accept that or not."

Excuse me? What did he mean by his "family's baby"? And what if it was a girl—was he saying they wouldn't love her? Who was this guy? My husband had been born and raised in this country. I certainly hadn't known he'd felt this way.

Sam continued, and I stared at him in silence, shocked. "Nadya is buying this stroller, and that's final."

"No, she's not! I refuse to use it. I don't want an orange clunky stroller."

"Well, that's fine, you don't have to use it."

I was perspiring, pregnant, and filled with rage. Nadya finally said something of benefit, likely because we had caused such a scene in the store by this point that everyone was staring at us to see what was going to happen next, and she was probably feeling the humiliation. She turned to the clerk and said, "I think we'll think about it and come back another time."

Sam stormed out of the store and got into the car. Nadya followed him and I followed her. Once we were in the car, nobody spoke. We drove to his parents' house in silence.

I realized on that drive that I had to leave him and take my baby with me. It was *not* his family's baby. I didn't care about anything else in that moment other than escaping. I just wanted out. I needed out. Where was I going to go?

We arrived at his parents' house, and his mother answered the door.

"Does my grandson have a stroller?" she asked us cheerfully. She noticed the expressions on our faces. "What happened?"

"I'm tired. I really need to go home," I said.

"Why don't you use your room here and get some rest?"

Oh, great—"our" room. Sam's parents had built a large bedroom, washroom, and living room in the basement for me and Sam. It was a genuinely kind—and costly—gesture, but it was not happening. Aside from the fact that they lived in the suburbs, there was no way in hell that I was living with my in-laws and in their basement. It was a common custom in Indian culture, but it had taken me completely by surprise. It had been, in fact, a surprise, a gift to us when we got married. Thankfully, Sam had no desire to live with his parents either, so he did the arguing for us. The basement remained unused, but my mother-in-law was holding out hope that we would move in eventually. She had thought that after the baby arrived we would stay with her for a while so that she could help out. We hadn't broken the news to her yet.

The polite gesture of telling me to rest in our room was not what I needed right now. "No!" I said, rather rudely. Nina looked surprised by my tone, and I immediately felt badly. She was trying so hard to help me, and even if she was a little overbearing, she didn't know what had happened and was always so kind to me. "Sorry, I'm just really tired, and I want to go home."

Sam said, "Well, you'll have to wait, because we are staying for dinner." It was only four o'clock—what did he mean staying for dinner? He wanted us to hang out at his mom's for a few hours after our huge argument? I truly was exhausted and needed a nap.

"Please take me home," I pleaded.

He looked at me and said, "Okay." He didn't say a word to his mother or his sister; he just walked out of his parents' house and toward the car and got in the driver's seat. I said bye to Nina and Nadya quietly and then got in the car. We drove home in silence during what seemed like the longest drive ever.

18

I opened the suitcase, put it next to my closet, and just started tossing things in. I couldn't even focus on whether things matched or would fit me. As I went into the bathroom to grab my toiletries, Sam said firmly, "Where the hell do you think you are going?"

"Does it matter? We are not working. This is not working. I am having a baby, your baby, and you care more about your sister and your mother than me."

Sam's voice rose as he said, "You're acting crazy."

"No, I'm not. Not only do they get to basically run my life, but on top of that, I don't see you doing much for us or this baby. I had to buy our baby's crib with my parents!"

I tossed my toiletry bag, hairbrush, and curling iron into my suitcase. I looked at my shoes, but I was wearing flip-flops because my swollen feet wouldn't fit into anything else. The ones I was wearing were enough. I zipped up my suitcase, hauled it up, and grabbed my purse.

As I walked toward the door, Sam said, "Tell me where you're going. You are carrying my child. I have a right to know!"

"Oh, *now* it's your child; *now* you want to have something to do with this baby?" I opened the door and walked out.

The elevator arrived quickly, which never happened, since we were on the penthouse level. I got in and felt relieved to be out of that hostile environment but completely freaked out. Where was I going? My parents had taken off to Vancouver to start checking out new homes, and they had left the keys to their house with the agent. I couldn't possibly stay there, with all the staged furniture and people coming and going for showings. How awkward for prospective buyers to see me there, and I'd probably have to leave every time there was an open house or people coming through. Besides, if my parents found out I had left, they would probably hop on a plane and come back. I didn't want to do that to them. I couldn't stay with friends; I was so heavily pregnant that they would have no idea what to do with me. I decided I was going to my aunt's house in Markham. She had space, and she wouldn't mind at all. My mom's sister was like a second mother to me, and her kids were more like my siblings than my cousins.

When I arrived at my aunt's house, she was sitting on the front porch reading a book and sipping an after-dinner cup of tea. It was a hot August evening, and the sun was setting as I arrived. I had called her on the way to tell her that I was having a few issues with Sam and needed a few days to breathe. She'd said I could stay as long as I wanted.

As I walked up to the house, she got up from her chair and said, "It's so good to see you, sweetheart."

She opened her arms, and I walked right into them. I placed my head on her shoulder and whispered, "Thank you so much."

"Come sit down. It's a perfect evening to sit outside and breathe in that summer air that we just don't get enough of."

She was right; it was a perfect evening. We savored every minute of every warm day in Toronto because we just didn't have enough of them. My aunt and I shared a love of the heat.

We sat there in quietness. She offered me water from a jug with lemon slices floating in it. "That would be great. Thanks." She passed me the glass of water, I sipped it, and then I put it down on the side table, beside her teacup. "I can't do this," I said.

"Can't do what? From where I'm sitting, you are married to a man who adores and spoils you, you are about to have a beautiful baby, which is the greatest gift one can get, and you have just finished an extremely competitive educational program that will only mean amazing things to come."

Wow, talk about perspective. I stared at her, shocked by how my aunt had summarized my life, because it certainly didn't seem as fabulous as she made it sound.

"I think you have forgotten about my mother-in-law, my sister-in-law, the fact that Sam doesn't lift a finger, the fact that all my friends have started working and I'm at home, pregnant, with no idea what my future holds."

My aunt listened and said, "I think what you need is a good night's sleep. You look tired, and figuring out solutions to all these issues that aren't actually issues, in my opinion, is not going to happen this evening."

She was right; I was exhausted. We walked upstairs, and she reminded me that I would be sharing a double bed with my nineteen-year-old cousin Zara, who was at her summer job, waitressing at a nearby restaurant, and wouldn't be home for a few more hours. She was only a few years younger than me, but she seemed a lot younger. Six years is a lot when you're growing up.

My uncle brought my suitcase upstairs, and I brushed my teeth, changed into a T-shirt and boy shorts, and got into my teenage cousin's bed. I fell asleep almost as soon as my head hit the pillow.

I opened my eyes and found myself staring directly at Zara, who was in bed beside me.

"Hi," she said before erupting into giggles.

"Hi," I replied, returning her giggle.

"So what the hell are you and this big belly doing in my bed? I can't believe I'm sharing my bed with a pregnant woman." She could barely get the words out through her laughter. I grabbed the pillow from under her and swatted her firmly over the head. "Thanks," she said. "Real mature. Seriously, though, are you okay?"

It felt good to be with my cousin, but at the same time I knew this was not where I should be. I could give birth any minute, and lying beside my teenage cousin instead of my husband wasn't right.

"I just needed to escape him. He doesn't care about me. All he wants to do is please his family, and he hasn't done anything to get ready for this baby."

"Is that what you really think? He adores you. He tells everyone, whether they want to listen or not, how much he loves you. That boy wanted you for years, and you wanted him, and you both finally got it together to make things work out. Now you just want to throw it away? He cares about his mom and sister and probably just hasn't figured out how to balance everything yet. What do you expect? Neither of you were planning on a baby at this point. Guys take time to adapt."

Was my baby cousin actually giving me advice? She was making sense, which shocked me. Maybe she wasn't a baby after all.

"Well, are you going to say anything?" she asked.

"I have to pee, like right now." We started laughing again, and then I rolled out of bed, making a thud as I hit the ground, and hobbled to the washroom.

I wheeled my suitcase through the door. The condo was empty. Sam must have gone to work. I walked in and sat on the sofa, not sure what to do with myself. I was suddenly so uncomfortable. I decided to go for a walk and maybe get an herbal tea at the Soho hotel, which was a short walk from my condo. I'd have to go alone, since my friends from law school were already busy working hard at their new jobs. They had started working as soon as we had completed the bar exam, and I was certain that if I'd asked them to lunch, they'd all have lots of interesting stories to tell me. Although I was genuinely excited for them, I couldn't handle talking to them right now. I was supposed to be working at a law firm downtown, busting my ass to prove my worth to some arrogant senior partner, but instead, here I was, pregnant and trying to fill my day with something other than worrying about what would become of me, of my career, of the life I'd so desperately wanted to start working toward.

I drank my tea, distracting myself by wondering when this baby would come. Today, tomorrow, next week? I needed my little baby to come out so I could start working on getting this body back into shape.

LEIA LONDON

As I made my way out, I looked at the window full of decadent desserts. The chocolate blackout cake and the almond strawberry shortcake were by far my favorite choices, which meant that, although everything else looked equally tempting, I would never taste them. Just like with breakfast, I couldn't help but get my favorites. I ordered a small strawberry shortcake for pickup the next day and then went home.

19

To settle my nerves while I waited for Sam to come home, I decided to make dinner. As I was chopping vegetables for a chicken stir-fry, he walked in.

"You're back!" he said. I'd thought he was going to be upset, but he wasn't. In fact, he seemed really happy. He came up to me and wrapped his arms around me, pulling me close, and whispered in my ear, "Don't ever leave me. We can work things out."

This was not at all what I'd expected. Apparently, my aunt had texted him to say that I was fine and not to worry, so I guess that had helped.

We ate dinner together, and I explained how uncomfortable I was and how I just wanted the baby to come out.

I was just about thirty-eight weeks, and the obsession had set in—I could no longer handle pregnancy. Of course, I really hadn't liked being pregnant over the entire course of my pregnancy, but it had at least been bearable until now. I hated it most when people told me to enjoy my pregnancy. What was there to enjoy? The initial fatigue and morning sickness? Rushing to the washroom every five minutes? The constant fear of stretch marks forcing me to slather all sorts of potions and lotions over my belly, hips, and thighs? Or was it staring at all the beautiful clothes in my wardrobe and wondering if I would ever fit into them again?

I could no longer bear these thoughts. My mind was consumed with getting the baby out. I felt so damn heavy, and scrolling through pictures friends had posted from the summer didn't help—my face and arms were a lot larger than I'd ever seen them. I couldn't handle my body, my constant fatigue, and playing the waiting game.

In our birth preparation class, we'd discussed methods of induction. At this point no doctor would aid in my desire for induction because I was not yet overdue, so I would have to resort to natural methods. I began recounting what we'd learned in class.

I could have sex because semen contains a hormone that induces labor. I was certain that Sam would be excited by my proposition, since we hadn't had sex in a while, but he'd also be suspicious. I'd read somewhere that some people encounter a second honeymoon during their second trimester because of the increased energy after the constant sickness of the first trimester. There might be other reasons involved too, but I didn't know because it hadn't happened to me—which was kind of funny, since that was the one thing my husband had actually known about pregnancy. He'd been told by one of his friends that I would have an increased libido, but that was quite the opposite of what I'd felt. Some nights he would snuggle up really close and give me little kisses—his hint of what he wanted—but I'd shuffle away: my hint that he wasn't going to get any action. After a few rejections, he'd stopped trying. I couldn't remember the last time we'd had sex. I'd have to come clean.

After we cleared the table, we sat on the sofa and I put my head in his lap. I looked up at him with a little grin and asked, "Would you like to have sex?"

He smiled. Yes, I thought. I was definitely going to get this baby out, and he was going to help me. In just a little while my contractions would start. It would only be a matter of time before this baby would be out of me. I was so excited.

"Why do you want to have sex right now? I mean, aren't you scared of hurting the baby, or, well, don't you feel weird that the baby is almost ready to come out? I don't think we should. We haven't had sex for so long, we might as well wait a little longer."

Was my husband seriously rejecting me? How could he? Maybe he was no longer attracted to me!

Actually, I didn't care if he was no longer attracted to me; I had an ulterior motive, and it wasn't to feel desired. I couldn't give up. I needed his help to fulfill my objective.

"Samir, I need to have sex."

"What do you mean you need to have sex?"

"Don't you remember in our class we learned that sex induces pregnancy? The same thing that got me pregnant can help end this pregnancy by inducing labor. It would also be helpful if I had an orgasm, because my uterus will contract, which may kick-start contractions," I explained.

"Are you crazy? You should hear yourself. Anyway, now that I've heard everything you have to say, we are definitely not having sex."

"But you don't know how I feel! I feel like crap! I need this baby to come out."

"The baby will come out when he is ready to come out. What if you induce labor and then the baby is not healthy because he wasn't ready? Wouldn't you feel terrible? Things will happen as they're supposed to happen."

He had just crushed my plans. Well, I would find other ways if he wasn't going to help me. I thought back to the class and remembered something about nipple stimulation. I barely had any sensation in my nipples, so how would that work, or did it matter? I didn't think it was possible anyway, because I remembered reading that it had to be performed for a few hours a day over a few days.

There was no way I was going to get Sam to help me with that one, nor was I going to do it to myself.

Sam got up to take Versace, whom we'd inherited from my parents when they'd staged their house, out for his walk.

"Can you buy a pineapple for me from the grocery store?" I asked. I hoped that he would assume it was merely a pregnant woman's craving, and apparently he did, because he agreed. Before he left, I said, "It has to be fresh, not canned."

"Okay, fresh pineapple. Got it."

He did indeed come home with a pineapple. I was impressed.

"So can you cut it for me?"

"No, I don't know how."

"Well, I don't really know how either."

"Why don't you call my mom and ask her how?"

Why did he always have to bring up his mother? As if I would call her randomly and ask her how to cut a pineapple. If I called her, then I'd have to explain everything, which I didn't feel like doing. I couldn't call my parents because they were at a wedding. I could call one of my aunts—oh, forget it, I would just try to do it myself. How hard could it be? I loved pineapple and ate it often, but I'd just never cut it up myself.

I managed to butcher it into bite-size pieces. Sam noticed that I was eating the pineapple rapidly and with conviction.

"Wow, you really wanted that pineapple, didn't you?"

I supposed I could confide in him now. I mean, I had already eaten about a third of it, so there was nothing he could do.

"You know how I really want this baby to come out?"

"Yeah."

"Well, apparently pineapple softens the cervix, which helps the baby move along or something like that. And guess what? You just helped me attempt to induce labor by buying the pineapple for me." I continued smiling, feeling so sly.

"You tricked me!"

"I did not. You never asked, and I never provided you with a reason, so there was no trickery involved," I proudly announced. I had won this round with Sam. Now to see if I'd won it with the baby.

A few hours passed, and I felt nothing.

I couldn't remember any other natural methods from class, so I Googled it. Soon the helpful information started flowing. Natural methods took a few hours to kick in, according to the research. I compiled a list of methods that didn't require Sam's help and organized it, starting with things that I would try immediately that didn't require too great an expense, and that were least harmful to my body, at least in my opinion.

First I started with cumin tea. I'd read that one tablespoon of cumin in a cup of hot water was thought to induce labor. The website had suggested adding sugar or honey to make it palatable, which I would definitely do. I stirred up the concoction and then sat on the sofa, sipping the drink from my mug. It was like drinking a watery curry. At least I was used to the flavor.

Naturally, Sam asked what I was drinking.

"Selena, the baby will come when he's ready. Don't force him out." I found it funny that he sounded just like Dr. Robinson had all those months ago, when he'd doubted her.

That night when I went to bed, the baby moved around a lot. Maybe tonight would be the night...

20

On the morning I awoke with my tummy feeling even heavier. I had to move. I could take the dog for a long walk, but that would be too much. I needed incentive. The cake! That delicious, fluffy almond-strawberry shortcake was ready to be picked up.

I rolled over to my side, slowly, and slid my legs off the bed to get up. When I stood up, I felt the blood rush to my feet, as if they were swelling instantly. Of course, I couldn't actually observe this happening, since I couldn't see over my large belly, but I could most certainly feel the sensation. I could also feel my bladder, which was telling me to rush to the washroom or else it wasn't going to be pretty.

As I got ready, I started to feel faint, pinching pains in my side. Was this the baby kicking? Was this a stretch mark forming? Who knew at this point? I stuffed my feet into flip-flops and texted Sam to tell him I was heading out to pick up the cake as I was trying to ignore the pain. I didn't usually text him when I was going out, but given that I was at the end of my pregnancy, I just thought that was what I was supposed to do. Almost instantly he replied with "okay."

As I walked the two blocks to the Soho—slowly—I started to feel a little achy in my lower back. The hot sun felt like it was sitting on top of my head. Normally I loved the sunshine and heat, but today it was unbearable. I tried to walk quickly, since all I wanted to do was go home and sit down, but my legs wouldn't move any faster.

Somehow I managed to pick up the cake and get back home without losing hope. I placed the pretty cake box on the top shelf of the fridge, bargaining with myself. Normally I'd wait to share it with company or at least Sam, but I didn't think I could wait that long this time. I was already craving it. I told myself I could have a slice after lunch, and I closed the fridge door. Then the pain in my side hit me again, but this time it hurt more, like period cramps. It had been months since I'd felt that kind of pain. Which meant...

Wait a second—was this happening?

My phone rang. I looked at the screen and saw that it was my mom.

"Hi, Ma!" I said with as much enthusiasm as I could muster standing in my kitchen in a state of utter confusion and total discomfort.

"Hi, sweets! Just wanted to let you know that we finished with the wedding in Calgary. The *mehndi* and *sangeet* parties were held together the day before the wedding. The bride's hair and makeup were gorgeous. Too bad she lives in Calgary, or I would have gotten the names of the ladies who made her look so beautiful." My mom continued to discuss the wedding in great detail, while I sort of listened and paced. The discomfort in my back and my stomach seemed to have gone, at least. My mom finally concluded her story by saying, "We fly in tomorrow, so make sure not to have the baby before then." She giggled as if she'd meant it as sarcasm.

"Well, actually, Ma, I'm starting to feel really crampy, and it's kind of different than anything I've felt. I'm also getting periodic low back pain."

There was silence at the other end of the phone. My mom was clearly trying to process this information.

"It may be the start of labor. See how you are feeling, and just don't have the baby before we get there. We wanted to be at the brunch they had for family and out-of-town guests today. It would have been rude if we hadn't stayed, and there are no flights from Calgary to Toronto this evening, so we're stuck flying out tomorrow. What am I saying? Look, it's your first baby. Labor is a long process, especially the first time. I'm sure you holding it in combined with this being your first will certainly buy us time."

"Okay, Ma, I'll call you later," I said quickly, hanging up before she could continue with her crazy talk. What did she mean by "holding it in"? First of all, I wanted nothing more than to get this baby out, and second, even if I wanted to hold it in, was that even possible?

My phone lit up with a text from my cousin Jay:

"I'm downtown meeting a friend for brunch and just finished. Are you home? I'm five minutes away if you are up for company."

Jay, who was Zara's brother, was like a brother to me. He was two years younger, which wasn't a lot, but given that I was married, having a baby, and living in my own home, it suddenly felt like I was way ahead of him in the game of life.

"Come up!" I texted back.

When Jay came in, he said, "Wow, you look like you're ready to pop!"

"Thanks," I said sarcastically as I hugged my cousin. "I haven't been feeling well today. I woke up this morning feeling cramps." As I said this, I was hit with another one, and I rubbed the side of my stomach to soothe the discomfort.

Jay stared at me and smiled. "Uhhh...sooo...do you want me to call someone?" Then we both started laughing. He was not comfortable and clearly not sure what the heck to do. "Seriously, Selena, are you in labor?" he asked.

"I don't think so. Well, maybe. I don't know. It's not like I've been in labor before."

"Well, have you timed these pains? That's what they do on TV."

As ridiculous as that sounded, he was right.

"No, I haven't timed them. Do you have a watch?"

"Who wears a watch these days, Sel? I've got my phone. Okay, tell me when you start feeling something."

"Now! Well, I think I feel something. It's like a faint pain. Okay, it's gone."

"That didn't seem like it could be a contraction. It was so short, like only a few seconds."

"I think it's supposed to be short, and then they get longer and happen more frequently."

Jay frowned at me. "Didn't you take lessons or read up on this stuff? Why are you guessing about labor when you may actually be in labor?"

"Jay, calm down." I couldn't believe he was lecturing me. "I don't think there is a step-by-step labor guidebook."

"Well, let's Google it, then. I bet we can find a YouTube video and an online guide and so much more, because clearly you don't know how to have a baby."

"Wait, start the timer, having another one!"

By the time we'd gone through this four more times, Jay and I realized this was the real deal.

The keys in the front door interrupted my thoughts. Sam came into the kitchen and gave Jay one of those bro handshake/hug things.

"How's it going, man?" he asked Jay. Sam loved company. He loved having our home filled with people, so seeing Jay there put a big smile on his face.

LAW GIRL'S BUMP IN THE ROAD

"It's all good," Jay said, "but your wife is about to have a baby."

"Yeah, I noticed," Sam said. "It's crazy. Could happen any day."

"No, I don't think you get it. She is about to have the baby now."

Sam looked at me. "What? Why didn't you call me? What's going on?"

"I may not be having the baby. I'm just getting these little pains in my—" It happened again. Sam and Jay stared at me as I bent over, trying to relieve the discomfort in my stomach.

Sam said, "Okay, let's get out of here. We need to go to the hospital now." He went into the bedroom and grabbed the suitcase I had packed a week ago.

"We aren't supposed to go to the hospital until the contractions are close together, or they will just send us home." I started to put the dishes from the sink into the dishwasher. "Sam, take the trash out to the garbage chute. And Jay, can you take the dog with you?" They both stared at me. "What's the issue, guys? I'm not leaving the condo a mess so that I can come home to a mess with a baby!"

Sam complied and took the garbage out. Jay picked up Versace's rhinestone-bedazzled leash and chuckled.

"Seriously, Sel. How am I supposed to look like a straight guy walking a shih tzu with all this bling?"

I smiled and was about to reply when I had a sudden surge of pain and keeled over. "Maybe we should go to the hospital," I gasped.

Sam and Jay stepped into action, Sam grabbing the suitcase (after I made him wash his hands properly) and Jay grabbing the dog and assuring us they'd be fine. As the elevator doors opened in the parking garage, Sam grabbed my hand and said, "Selena, I love you." I instantly gained so much strength. I was ready.

At the hospital, Sam let me out and said he would go find parking and bring up my suitcase while I went to the maternity ward.

"I'm in labor," I whispered to the middle-aged woman in scrubs at intake.

She stared at me. "Dear, is this your first?"

"Yes," I replied.

"Labor is a multistep process. You may not actually be at the part of labor when you come to the hospital. You look okay."

I felt like the nurse was trying to turn me away. I wasn't lying; I was in labor! I didn't have the strength to argue, so I just stood there feeling stupid.

Finally, she took me to a room behind the desk that was divided with curtains and handed me a hospital gown.

I stared at it, wondering which way was the front and which was the back.

"Excuse me," I called to the nurse. "Can I wear my own nightie?"

"No, dear, just put on the one I gave you," she said firmly.

Where was Sam? I didn't want to be alone in this place any longer. I lay down on the bed, and another woman came in.

"Hi there, I'm Dr. Joy! Yes, that is my real name," she said with a smile. "I'm going to check your cervix to see how many centimeters you are at. If you are less than three centimeters, then normally we ask you to come back later, but let's not get ahead of ourselves."

This doctor was so much friendlier than the intake nurse, at least. But then she spread my legs open, and oh geez, was this happening? Was that an object she was sticking up there, or maybe her fingers? I had no idea, but it wasn't coming out.

"Just relax," Dr. Joy said. Relax? There was something in me down there, and things were hooked up to my chest and my arm, and I was getting severe cramps in my tummy. There was no way I could relax. And where was Sam?

Dr. Joy took out whatever she'd put in me and smiled. "You're between four and five centimeters! Let's get you checked in immediately."

The curtain swung open, and it was Sam, staring at my fully exposed down-there area and the doctor, who was sitting on a stool between my spread-open legs.

"Sam, close the curtain!" I yelled.

"Sorry, Sel. I didn't know you were going to be flashing everyone. Kinda looks messy down there and swollen. Do things go back to normal, or is it always going to look all big and mushy down there?"

Dr. Joy laughed, but I was raging. "Sam, seriously?"

The doctor explained the next steps, and then another nurse came into the room. She looked like she was about my age, and she had a very excited demeanor.

"Hello! I'm Ashley. I'll be with you through your labor. I've got a birthing room ready for you, so let's walk you over."

The birthing room was better than I'd expected. It had a private washroom and a sofa for Sam. As I sat on the bed, I asked Ashley for the anesthesiologist, and she left to make the call.

As she walked out of the room, Sam said, "I thought we were going to try natural?"

"We are having this baby naturally. It's coming out the same hole that this situation started in, but I'm doing it with meds. Sam, I can barely manage the pain right now."

"You seem fine," he replied.

"Well, I'm on the verge of not managing, and we could have several more hours of this pain."

He opened his mouth to say more when suddenly his mom, dad, and sister appeared in the doorway. What were they doing here?

Sam avoided my gaze and went to greet them. I pulled my hospital gown tighter around me. I wasn't wearing underwear, the back of the gown was open, and I couldn't even close my legs all the way because of my big belly. This was so humiliating.

Nina approached me. "You don't look like you're in labor," she said.

"Well, I am." I didn't mean to be rude, but I was so uncomfortable and just wanted to be alone with Sam.

Luckily, Ashley came in and said, "Excuse me, but this is the birthing suite. Only Mom and one to two helpers can be present."

Oh no.

Nina said in a giddy voice, "I can be a helper!"

Was my mother-in-law actually going to stay? Was she going to see a baby come out of my private parts? This could not be happening.

Sam said, "Yeah, Mom! Great idea!"

Ashley looked at me, then turned to Nina. "Actually, the intake paperwork said the only helper is Sam, and Dr. Joy prefers just one helper and the nurse, which is me. Sorry about that. I forgot that it was Dr. Joy on rotation today."

Nina looked back at her. The stare-down was on. But Ashley's gaze did not waver. Ashley rocked!

Nina said bye to me and gave me a loose hug. She hugged Sam, who agreed to call her as soon as the baby arrived, and then she left to join her daughter and husband. Sam seemed clueless about what had just happened.

Ashley came over to tell me that the anesthesiologist would be down in a few minutes. Before she walked away, I grabbed her arm, looked into her eyes, and whispered, "Thank you." She smiled, aware of what I was thanking her for, and walked away.

Dr. Joy appeared in the room next. "I believe we should break your water."

"Isn't that supposed to happen at a restaurant or in the hallway and make a big mess, like in the movies?" Sam asked curiously.

"In real life, not always." Dr. Joy split my legs apart again, and Sam looked away, apparently not wanting to see the situation down there.

"Ouch!" I blurted out as another object was stuck into me. All of a sudden, I felt a gush of warm liquid pouring out of me. "What is happening?"

"We just broke your water. Things will move along much quicker now." Dr. Joy and Ashley cleaned everything up and left.

The pain was so brutal. I turned to my left, then to my right, but there was no relief. Every minute, I felt flushed and then started to feel like I was going to vomit, but I didn't. There was just more pain. The clock in the room gave me anxiety, since I knew that on cue the pain would return. Where was the damn anesthesiologist?

Ashley returned. "I can't take this any longer!" I whimpered. "Please tell me the anesthesiologist is coming. I need drugs now!"

In came another doctor. "Hi, I'm Dr. David. Let's go through this list of questions, and then I can set you up with the perfect drug cocktail."

A "perfect drug cocktail" was exactly what I wanted.

Sam chimed in as we went through the questions, while I quickly answered no to every question about my medical history and allergies and such.

"I'm not so sure about this drug cocktail," Sam said. "We're thinking about a natural birth."

Dr. David and I stared at Sam. "I want it, and I want it now," I said through gritted teeth as another contraction came.

Dr. David and Ashley helped me up, and I leaned over the bed as Ashley held my hands on the other side. I knew I couldn't move or else. I felt another contraction coming, this one stronger and harder. I told myself, Don't move, don't move. I could feel the perspiration forming on my forehead, and then I felt a stab in the back, literally. It was so brutal. I was in so much pain in my stomach and now in my back, but I could not move. Sam had left the room as soon as he'd seen the needle.

"All done," announced Dr. David. I released Ashley's hands from my own and realized how hard I had been squeezing them.

"I'm so sorry. I hope I didn't hurt you," I said.

She smiled. "Not to worry. That was nothing compared to some women!" She helped me into the bed. Dr. David gave me a remote connected to the IV and instructed me to press the button anytime I felt the numbness wearing off.

Really? That's it? I was done with the pain? Yay! I was so happy it was over, and why I'd had to endure the pain of contractions up to that point made no sense to me.

The next three hours went by quickly and were a bit of a blur. A nurse got upset at me for eating Twizzlers because I wasn't supposed to eat anything in case I needed an emergency C-section. I told the nurse that I was absolutely not having a C-section, so she didn't need to worry about my Twizzler consumption. The nurse rudely confiscated my Twizzlers.

Aside from the Twizzler incident, I read magazines and then dozed off. Our phones weren't working in the birth room, another bunkerlike situation, I guessed. Sam wasn't in the room much because he was in an area of the hospital where he could get cell reception so he could call, text, and post on social media the news that we were at the hospital. I didn't care to participate in sharing the news. I liked that this was a private moment for us to savor before our lives changed forever. Sam called my mom and was told to relay the message, "Hold it in; we'll be there in the morning." I dozed off peacefully.

It was 11:05 p.m. when I awoke because of pressure in my lower abdomen. What was that? It wasn't going away. Was my epidural wearing off? No, it wasn't pain; it was pressure. Ashley was in the room reading the heart monitor. I looked at her and said, "Something is happening. I feel something weird, like a pressure down on my tummy."

She placed her hand on the lower part of my tummy. "It's time!" she announced with a smile. Time? Like *that* time? Now what?

Ashley rushed out of the room and returned with Sam and Dr. Joy. Ashley stood on my right side and told Sam to stand on my left. They were each holding one leg back while Dr. Joy focused down there.

"When the next contraction comes, you'll need to push. You can't tell because of the epidural, so I'll tell you when. Okay, now! Push!" she said.

I pushed as hard as I could, trying desperately to stay calm and loose. I didn't want to tear.

"Wow, you are an expert pusher! I'm surprised that this is your first child."

I was skeptical. "I'm sure you say that to everyone."

"No, I'm serious, you're only going to need a few pushes like that. I can see the head already."

My expression probably showed that I wasn't buying it. I thought people were supposed to push for hours. I had pushed only once, and this doctor was trying to tell me she could see the head? I also wasn't screaming and panting and doing all that stuff that you see on television. Yeah right, a few more pushes.

"How about I bring in a mirror so you can see what I'm seeing?"

Wow, they could do that? "That's a fantastic idea. Thank you so much!" Ashley rushed out of the room.

Sam was not liking that idea. "Selena, do we have to get a mirror? I don't want to see what's going on down there. How do you expect me to ever be in that area again, seeing all this stuff happening and coming out of you?"

Ashley wheeled in a long mirror, and then she resumed her position, holding back my right leg. We all ignored Sam's comments on the mirror.

Dr. Joy was right. Two more pushes and the baby was out. And I got to see it actually happening for myself.

Suddenly, a baby with steel-gray eyes and a full head of dark hair was placed on my chest. This baby, who seconds ago had been inside me, was now on top of me. Was I dreaming?

As I stared at my baby and placed my arms around him, nothing else mattered. My concerns over the last few months seemed so trivial and so distant from my mind. I was in love in a way that I had never felt in my entire life. I desperately wanted to take care of this little boy, protect him, and give him everything I could. This was my son.

I stared into his eyes, and he grasped my finger with his entire hand. My eyes welled up with tears as I gazed at our precious little boy. I whispered something that merely minutes ago I would never have expected would come out of my mouth.

"The last few months weren't so bad. I think I could do it again."

About the Author

Leia London is an attorney and mother of three living in Toronto. She was inspired to write *Law Girl's Bump in the Road* during her first pregnancy. While based on a true story, the novel is an entertaining and lighthearted yarn in the vein of *The Devil Wears Prada* and Sophie Kinsella's Shopaholic series.

Made in the USA
Columbia, SC
14 February 2018